EARTHQUAKE 2099

Other books by Mary W. Sullivan

WHAT'S THIS ABOUT PETE?
THE VW CONNECTION

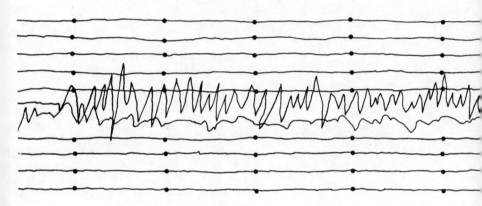

EARTHQUAKE 2099

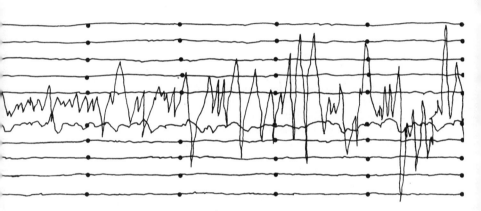

Mary W. Sullivan

LODESTAR BOOKS

E. P. Dutton   New York

LIBRARY OF CONGRESS CATALOGING IN PUBLICATION DATA

Sullivan, Mary W.
    Earthquake 2099.

    Summary: Philip, whose eleven years have been spent in the controlled environment of an Urban Complex Tower, learns to survive among wild animals and wild people in the Wildlife Preserve after an earthquake.
    [1. Science fiction.   2. Earthquakes—Fiction.   3. Survival—Fiction]
I. Title.   II. Title: Earthquake two thousand ninety-nine.
PZ7.S9533Ear   1982   [Fic]   82-7128
ISBN 0-525-66761-X   AACR2

Published in the United States by E. P. Dutton, Inc., 2 Park Avenue, New York, N.Y. 10016. Published simultaneously in Canada by Clarke, Irwin & Company Limited, Toronto and Vancouver.
Editor: Virginia Buckley   Designer: Trish Parcell
Printed in the U.S.A.   First Edition
10 9 8 7 6 5 4 3 2 1

to my daughter and friend, Molly Sullivan

Contents

1
Good-bye, Towers

A welter of kids, mostly in blue-and-gold soccer uniforms, poured out of Philip's farewell party. Pushing and shoving, they moved toward the elevator on the 209th floor of Golden Spires Urban Complex Tower 117 on the far edge of the North Continent.

Before piling into the elevator, Philip's friends all told him good-bye, some adding things like: "Don't let the wild animals eat you!" Ariel, the girl he liked best, said, "Be careful."

Philip couldn't bear to say good-bye, but he kept smiling. All he managed to say was "See you" over and over, even though he had no idea if he'd ever see any of them again.

When the elevator door at last slid shut, the tears he'd been holding back blurred his eyes. He turned, head down, and stumbled blindly into his own apartment. He wanted to really bawl like a little kid. How could he give up his friends? All his life—his entire eleven years—he had spent with them as they grew up together in Tower 117. As he closed the door behind him, he heard his mother's voice. "I know it's hard, Philip. But believe me, you will love it. And—"

"Mom! You'll never persuade me. But I'm going anyway. I'm all packed."

His mother patted his shoulder. "I wasn't trying to persuade you. It's too late for that. Dad's waiting on the roof. But I have news for you. Your cousin Vita is coming up from the Open Country to stay with us in the Preserve. She'll be company for you, like a big sister."

Philip glared through his tears. "I don't want a big sister! I don't want any sister. I like it just fine the way things are right here." Philip could count on one hand the number of times he'd left the Towers. Four times the soccer team had been taken by aerobus to play teams in other Towers. Once his whole class had been flown out over the ocean and the outer islands to where they could see the wall that separated them from the Open Country, as well as some of the Open Country itself. Each time they had all been glad to come home to the controlled environment of Tower 117, where they felt safe.

Now his parents had accepted an assignment on the seashore, seventy-six kilometers north of the Towers. They were to take a count of the plants and animals in the Shark Tooth Mountain Wildlife Preserve. And they wanted Philip to go, too.

He sighed. "I said I'd go. And I will go." He tried to conquer his misgivings, but he had to ask. "So what if I get sick breathing the outside air? You don't even care."

His mother laughed. "Don't worry. You won't get sick. Acid smog is a thing of the past." She picked up her bag and stood by the door.

Philip scowled at her. Then he snatched up his gear, slung it across his shoulder, and ran ahead. To let his mother know that he was still angry, he kicked the panel that summoned the elevator.

When the door slid open, he and his mother took their places in front of the other passengers. As they rose, Philip peered through the glass walls for a last look at the floors that had meant so much to him: Floor 210, where he had gone to school; Floor 211, where the kids hung out by the lake in the little park after school, to drink instanutri-shakes and eat honeygurt cones.

They had to stand aside on Stadium Floor 212, while all of the other passengers pushed out to pick up tickets for Sunday's soccer match.

Philip groaned as the door closed. Scenes of games with his friends crowded into his mind—kids running, tumbling together on the turf, kicking the black-and-white ball, butting it with their heads.

In a kind of replay, he suddenly felt himself jolted—flung onto one knee. What was happening? The elevator lurched from side to side.

"Mom!" he screamed.

His mother staggered against him. They clung together in a desperate attempt to keep their footing. Philip's heart flip-flopped as he stared, speechless, into his mother's panicked eyes.

Then the lights went out, and the elevator began to fall. In total darkness, they plunged down and down. Philip's insides felt torn loose—unable to drop so swiftly. Terrified, he clung to his mother.

Abruptly, they stopped. For a moment the elevator hung suspended, its lights blinking on and off. Philip's stomach seemed to rise into his chest.

Again it plunged.

And again it stopped.

Then, as if nothing had happened, the lights came back on.

Philip's scrambled insides adjusted as he felt himself lifted in the usual swift rise toward the roof.

"Whew!" he breathed, as his body went limp with relief.

"J-just a t-tremor," his mother said in an unsteady voice. "We haven't had one of those in a long, long time." Philip gulped, his heart pounding. "You mean that was an earthquake?"

"Yes." She picked up her bag and grabbed his hand, ready to leave the moment the door flashed open on the roof level. "Let's get out of here!"

Dodging people, they ran onto the glass-enclosed airdrome. From there they could see the deck crowded with aerocars, aerotrucks, and buses.

Philip's voice came out high and scared-sounding. "W-will there b-be another quake?"

His mother didn't turn. Instead her eyes searched the outside deck. "Who knows? There is no way of telling. Come on, Philip! Hurry up!" She gestured with her head. "There's Dad."

Philip trembled as he followed her through the air locks that brought him into the unfamiliar outside air. Here people were rushing about trying to board aerocars and buses. The deck seemed to be swaying. Or were the Towers that loomed around him moving?

He didn't have time to find out.

"Dad!" he yelled as he neared the yellow aerocar. "Did you feel the quake?"

"Yes! Yes! Of course! Get in!" His father hustled them into their seats, and his mother pulled the lever that connected them to Central Power.

Immediately a humming sound began behind them as a plastic bubble rose over their heads. At almost the same time, a buzz on a lower note started the rotor shooting up to open above them like an umbrella.

4

The instant the humming stopped, Philip's mother pulled the other lever. It was marked *P*, and connected their aerocar with the Programmer. A green light flashed. His mother said, "Shark Tooth Mountain."

Philip held his watch to his ear. "The time is exactly three-ten and two seconds," said the electronic voice. Over and over his parents had told him that they would be living only nine minutes from the Towers.

Then the little aerocar tipped onto its rounded rear, rested there for a split second, and shot straight up out of the mass of Towers.

Again Philip's stomach acted up. But when he heard both of his parents heave sighs of relief, he relaxed, too, basking in the security of the aerocar's bubble.

His mother was describing their fright in the elevator. "We were lucky to get out of there alive," she told his father. "When the elevator lost its connection with Central Power, I thought we were done for. I wonder how bad the quake was."

"You won't have to wait long to find out. It will be on the news when we get there."

Now high in the sky, they had joined a glittering stream of air traffic. Beside them a red aerobus sailed silently along at the same speed. Ahead, Philip saw many aerocars, a few towing trailers coupled to them.

Glimmering far, far below, thin silver threads of the water system meshed squares of the great green-and-gold checkerboard croplands that sustained the Tower people. Away in the distance, beyond the wall that separated them, lay the parched brown land of the Open Country speckled with the dots that were crumbling houses. He glanced down again.

5

Before the Towers were built, there had been houses here, too. He wondered how it had looked then.

Now the aerocar began to go down, and his father leaned across him to study the ground below. "There! See?" He pointed to a gleaming speck that had to be the silver aerotrailer his parents had towed there. It sat all alone on a wide ledge halfway up a mountain bordered by the dazzle of endless sea.

It all looked exposed and open, Philip thought—nothing like the security of the Towers. How were they going to live down there? Where was everyone?

Philip's heart sank as the aerocar descended.

2
Strange-Acting Animals

It was all Philip could do to keep from wrapping his arms over the top of his head for protection. Reluctantly he followed his parents out of the aerocar. The hot afternoon sun dazzled his eyes, penetrated his soccer uniform, and made him sweat as if he had spent hours chasing soccer balls. He was glad to go inside the aerotrailer.

Right away he felt at home there. Because the aerotrailer was plugged into the electricity of Central Power, it had the same controlled climate as the Towers. Everything else was much the same as the Towers, too. Just inside the sliding glass doors was a small living area facing the telewall, which, under the space for personal messages, continuously supplied the news.

Anxiously Philip and his parents stood together to read the printout: MINOR EARTHQUAKE JOLTS AREA. MINIMAL DAMAGE TO THE TOWERS. EPICENTER ON OPEN COUNTRY BORDER. BORDER WALL DOWN IN PLACES. PATROLS ALERTED. PARAMILITARY GROUP SCORPIONS THREATENS TO ASSUME CONTROL OF BORDER.

"Oh, no!" Philips's mother cried. "I thought they'd jailed all the Scorpions."

"Afraid not," his father said. "Just the ones caught executing those starving refugees."

"Dad," Philip asked, "what is a paramilitary group?"

His father looked worried. "An outlaw army of people who have chosen to take the law into their own hands. In this case they're an ignorant, underground bunch from the Towers that are bent on wiping out the people of the Open Country. They want to make that land as efficent as the Towers. They've infiltrated the Open Country, and it is said they have a hidden arsenal there. Most of them can speak the language of the Open Country."

Philip said, "I know some Open Country words. *Yi* means hello; *gada* means good-bye and *zogsi* is thank you. I'll say *yi* to Vita when she comes, but I wish it was *gada*."

His mother said, "Don't be funny, Philip. If you give her a chance, you might like her."

After he had stowed his gear in his tiny bedroom, Philip inspected the kitchen. He was hungry.

In the same arrangement as in the Towers, there was first the refrigerator, then the freezer on his right. Across from them was the counter with the insta-machine and, at the end, under the window, the sink. Philip took a gum-sized packet labeled "insta-burger" from the freezer and placed it under the bubble of the insta-machine, then watched it swell into a plump hamburger in a sesame-seed bun. When he lifted the lid, it smelled delicious, and he was happy to see that beside the hot burger and fries there lay a crunchy, cold apple.

He stuffed the apple in his pocket, left the fries on the counter, and grabbed his hamburger. While he ate he continued to inspect the kitchen. Why did it have those cupboards?

His father explained. "These aerotrailers provide space for emergency supplies: flashlights, matches, tools, extra water jugs."

"What's this stuff?" Philip pointed to a line of bags in the cupboard labeled "beans," then another labeled "corn flour."

"Flour and beans for Vita," his father told him.

Philip swallowed the last bite of his hamburger. "What kind of freak is she? Can't she eat insta-meals like the rest of us?"

"She's probably never seen an insta-meal. We want to do all we can to make her happy. But, turn around. There's something else I want to show you—our portable water system. Everything else here depends on electricity from Central Power, but not the water system."

Philip started on his apple as he followed his father to the little sink under the window in the kitchen. His father pointed up at the transparent tank overhead. "It uses solar energy to convert seawater into fresh water." He went on to explain, "With this chemical called Jonesite, it magnetizes the salt. And it's going to keep us pretty busy," he added. "Every day we'll have to hike to the beach to haul up water from the ocean. Things aren't as easy here as in the Towers."

He was right. Life in the Preserve wasn't easy or pleasant,

Philip thought. In the days that followed, if it hadn't been for this hauling of seawater, Philip might have spent all of his time inside the trailer watching soccer matches on the tele-wall, just so he wouldn't have to be out in that frightening wilderness climate.

He wouldn't even eat dinner outside at the picnic table with his parents. Instead, he ate his insta-meals in front of the telewall. Not even when his parents told him that they'd been feeding the little animals they had come to study, did he come out. "Don't push him," his father told his mother. "Give him time. It's a big adjustment."

Each day, smeared with sun screen and carrying two big plastic jugs, he followed his parents down the rocky trail to the beach. Where the trail's border of sun-bleached dry grass gave way to low brownish-green bushes, they often stopped to watch what seemed to be a tame rabbit. Sometimes it bounded out of the bushes right into their path.

To Philip it seemed exactly like a rabbit named Oscar that had been passed around from student to student in the third grade. Even though this one lived in the wild, its ears turned like Oscar's, and its nose and whiskers moved in what might be a signal that it wanted to be friends. Seeing Oscar was the only good part of the walk to the beach.

Beside the bushes where the rabbit lived, there were clumps of stickery green cactus. After a painful encounter with the cactus on the first day, Philip learned to avoid it and other thorny bushes. But he couldn't avoid the sea breeze that often brushed his skin and rumpled his hair. Or the warm sun that made him perspire in his soccer uniform. He was terrified of the sun. He knew it could burn his skin, and he tried to picture himself without skin.

His mother paid little attention to his complaints. "So," she shrugged as they walked down the trail. "If you're hot, why don't you take off your shirt or wear your swim trunks? I'll rub sun screen on you. When we get organized, I'm going to put on my suit and have a good long swim in the surf."

Philip was horrified. Suspiciously he looked at the waves crashing onto the beach. "You mean in there?" He knew that in the Open Country it was quite usual for people to bathe in the surf. But why risk drowning in the ocean when every floor of the Towers had a nice, safe pool?

On the beach, strands of greenish-brown seaweed clouded with tiny flies disgusted him. It took all of his courage to shed his soccer shoes and socks and wade far enough into the water to fill his jugs. Sand ground into the soles of his tender feet. The chill ocean bit at his legs, ankles and, now and then, unavoidably, his knees.

Once he found himself about to be swept off his feet when the sand churned away and the surf washed over his knees. A huge white breaker lifted out of the blue to loom above him. "Come back! Come back!" he screamed to the dark figures of his parents silhouetted against the wave's slick rise.

Instead of panicking, his parents tumbled with the wave to gather him up and scramble ashore. All the way home, hiking up the trail, wet and dripping, they laughed at his grumbling. "It's fun," they said. "We never guessed how much fun."

On the third day in the Preserve, they found a personal message on the telewall when they came up from the beach. VITA ARRIVING EIGHT TEN P.M. MARCH 23.

"Good!" Philip's mother said.

"Where do we meet her?" his father asked.

"At the border, I am sure."

Philip scowled. "Does she know any English at all?"

His mother shot back, "Judging by her phone call, it's better than yours."

"We're doing our share by having her come," explained his father. "The government has asked everyone who can to bring up any relative who survived the famine. We sent for my cousin Henry's offspring. As far as we're able to find out, Vita is his family's only survivor."

"Yeah, well," Philip couldn't knock that. Then he looked at the message on the telescreen to check the time. "Eight ten P.M. That's halfway through the match between our team and Tower 131! Don't ask me to go with you to meet Vita!"

His mother looked alarmed. "Are you sure you will be all right? We'll be gone for half an hour."

"Sure, I'll be okay. I probably won't move out of my chair."

His father agreed. "He'll be fine. What could happen in half an hour?"

So just after five minutes to eight on March 23, Philip sat comfortably watching the soccer match. Between mouthfuls of popcorn, he cheered his favorite player, Bernard Finch. Even though their team was behind, Bernard played well. But then he muffed a crucial play. Now the team was so far behind that there was no chance of catching up.

In disgust, Philip clicked the soccer picture off the telewall. He glanced at the words coming on the printout. REPORTS OF THE STRANGE BEHAVIOR OF ANIMALS ARE FLOODING INTO SEISMOLOGISTS' HEADQUARTERS. INCONCLUSIVE EVIDENCE HAS LONG REGARDED THIS AS AN EARTHQUAKE WARNING.

Philip leaped up. Earthquake warning! The walls seemed to close in on him, as if he were back in the elevator. No longer did the little aerotrailer seem secure. No way did he want to be trapped inside anything so small if another earthquake came. He raced outside.

Then he ran back in to get his popcorn and a flashlight. He would wait outside on the bench by the picnic table for his parents to come home.

But he felt strange there, too. The round white face of the moon seemed to be staring down at him, and the glittering stream of lights high in the sky that formed the aero-vehicles' sky path seemed unreal. He couldn't believe he had been up there. Would his parents really drop from the sky in the little yellow aerocar?

As if to prove that they would, something came hurtling out of the line. Larger than an aerocar, it seemed to be aimed straight at him. But, at the last moment, he saw that its destination was the beach below the trailer. The flashing lights of an aerobus dropped momentarily behind the bluff, then almost at once shot back into the sky.

Philip pressed the button on the side of his watch. "The time is exactly eight ten and twelve seconds," its canned voice announced. Eight ten! Vita was to be at the border at eight ten! Had there been some mix-up? Was she climbing up the path from the beach right now? He peered into the darkness. Should he go to meet her?

But what if it wasn't Vita? What if it was one of the Scorpions?

His body tensed at a rustling in the nearby bushes. He sat perfectly still, hoping he was hidden by the darkness. But the rustling continued and, reflecting the aerotrailer's lights, two shining disks glowed in the dark.

An animal! Philip turned his flashlight on a bushy little creature in a black bandit mask.

A raccoon! Keeping his flashlight on it, he cautiously

climbed onto the tabletop. He didn't want to scare it. But it might bite. How was he to know?

Another animal moved behind the raccoon. This one looked like a big, long-tailed rat.

An opossum.

Then Philip caught a glimpse of a black-and-white skunk with its tail held high.

As suddenly as the animals had come, they all vanished. Philip, trying to shine his light on them, climbed down from the table. But instead of spotting the animals, he caught sight of a figure hastening toward him.

It was a very thin person—only a little taller than he was. Too small for a Scorpion. It was a girl, and like Ariel, she was trim and fair-haired. But she dressed strangely, not at all like the energy-saving Tower people in their endurocloth gar-ments which never wore out. This girl wore a red plaid shirt and bluish pants, and she carried a large straw bag.

Vita! It had to be Vita.

He called out her name.

But instead of coming toward him, she hesitated and glanced back into the darkness before she asked, "Who is there?"

"Philip," he said. "*Yi!* I guess I'm your cousin or some-thing. Where are Mom and Dad? They went to meet you."

Without responding to his friendly "*yi,*" the girl set the straw bag on the ground beside her and tucked back a strand of fair hair that had escaped her braid. "I did not see them," she said.

"They went to the border. They are probably looking for you right now. How did you get here? Why didn't you wait for them?"

Vita shrugged. "I came on the aerobus. Your mother told

me you had moved to the wildlife preserve at Shark Tooth Mountain."

The eyes studying him looked to Philip like cold gray marbles, but he knew he should be nice to her. And he had to warn her about the earthquake. "Take your stuff inside. Then come back out. There may be an earthquake."

She stared. "An earthquake? Where did you get that idea?" Before he could explain, she picked up her bag and carried it inside.

Forget her, Philip told himself and turned to look for the animals.

He tossed them some of his popcorn and watched as they all gathered again. He didn't know much about animals, but he thought they were acting strange. They ran about the clearing moving uncertainly. The skunk circled, nose down. The raccoon ran a few feet, then stopped and rubbed its paws together. The opossum trundled worriedly. None of them seemed to be interested in his popcorn.

Was the earthquake going to happen right now?

Suddenly Philip knew that it was. A strange feeling had come over him, too. All of his senses came alive—he tingled from head to toe. Like the animals, he was getting the message of imminent danger.

The animals had banded together because of their fear. They knew the earthquake was coming. Philip knew it was coming. He needed someone, too. Why weren't his parents here?

He had no choice. There was no one else.

All he could do was scream, "Vita! Vita!"

3 Earthquake!

Then it happened. Philip's heart lurched as the earth jolted under him. His ears vibrated to a curious low crunching roar that rumbled throughout the dark bluffs. The whole world rocked, and he felt himself tossed away from the picnic table, onto his knees. Trying to find his bearings, he clung frantically to the dry grass in which he had landed. The lights on the aerotrailer reeled dizzyingly. They flared brighter, then faded away leaving him in the cold light of the spinning moon.

Not daring to rise from the shuddering earth, Philip crept toward the aerotrailer. "Vita!" he yelled. "Vita! Come help me!" But his voice seemed lost in the thundering of the sea, which now drowned out the earthquake's low roar.

Philip sprang to his feet. He saw that the aerotrailer was moving. As if driven by the malicious force that had taken control of the world, it lunged toward him.

He stumbled, turned, and ran. Clinging to bushes, he scrambled to safety up the heaving hillside just before the aerotrailer caromed off of it. As it passed him, he glimpsed Vita. Half in, half out, she was clutching the sides of the doorway. Her screams of terror penetrated the wild roar around them.

Philip answered her calls. But what could he do? With his arms wrapped around a bush, his eyes followed the aerotrailer. Now the earth seemed to tilt toward the sea. He hung on to the bush as rocks tumbled and crashed. The aero-trailer, its silver roof reflecting moonlight, plunged toward the edge of the bluff.

"Vita!" he screamed. "Jump! Jump!" Could she hear him? In the dim light he saw her terrified face framed in the aerotrailer's doorway. A few more feet and the aerotrailer would fall into the sea!

For an instant all sound diminished. The earth righted itself and Philip felt a surge of inner strength. He let go of the bush and ran to help Vita.

Before he could reach her, the world again went out of control. He lost his footing and sprawled on the ground. Again the aerotrailer headed for him. But, this time, the earth he lay on heaved him out of its way. Vita and the aerotrailer sailed past him, tilted over a newly formed knoll, and came to rest.

Philip shouted to her. A moment later she had climbed down from the aerotrailer and, outlined by moonlight, was walking uncertainly toward him. Sobbing, he ran to meet her.

Vita took his hands. For the moment, the rumbling had stopped. He was not alone. The one person left in his world was with him. He was safe. Vita was safe. The warmth of her hands comforted him. Softly, she said his name. "Philip, I am sorry I did not believe you. How did you know there was going to be an earthquake?"

Before he could answer, a boom far louder than the sea and earthquake came from the direction of the Towers. The evening sky turned to flame.

What was happening? What could cause an explosion of that magnitude—enough to blast eardrums even at a distance? Philip trembled because there was only one answer.

He turned to Vita. "Central Power! That blast must have been Central Power blowing up!"

She shook her head, and Philip saw that she didn't understand.

He tried to explain. "Without Central Power nothing will work! What will we do?" He remembered the prediction that this would happen in an earthquake severe enough to undermine Central Power's structure.

And the fiery sky! What did that mean? He knew, but his mind refused to accept the horror. It couldn't be, but it was. The Towers were burning—lighting the sky. His home was burning! His home and the home of all his friends! His friends—the soccer team, Bernard Finch, Ariel!

"Oh, Vita! Tell me that isn't the Towers. It can't be! It just can't be. And Mom and Dad! Where are they? I hope their aerocar landed safely."

He turned to her and felt comforted by the warmth of her arms around him. Then they were rocked again. A far more distant boom sounded to the north. The sky flamed briefly.

Hopelessly Philip shook his head and told Vita, "That is the Northern Power Plant, the backup to Central Power. Now it is gone, too."

Philip wanted to hide from this crazy world. But where was there to go? He looked toward the aerotrailer. Not there! The threatening sea thundered all too near. He turned toward the mountain above them. There he saw movement. Silhouetted against the bright sky, a doe and fawn bounded upward. Philip pointed. "Look, Vita. See those deer? Let's go up there. The animals may know where it is safe."

Vita seemed reluctant. Her eyes searched the mountainside, but she said okay, and they followed the deer. Disregarding small tremors, they stumbled forward. Halfway up, the earth's madness began again. They were thrown to the ground, where they felt heave after heave surge under them.

"Terrible!" Philip said as he held his unsettled stomach.

"Terrible!" Vita echoed.

What was happening to them was beyond words. For a moment Philip felt a sense of kinship toward Vita because they both had used the same word to describe their feelings. As they scrambled to their feet to climb again, they shook their heads and said the word over and over to each other.

What would they see from the top of the mountain? Could anything be more terrible than what they had already seen?

4 The Split-Off

Chilling gusts of wind, moist with salt spray, chased Philip and Vita up the last few meters of mountainside. Shivering, they peered down, at first not believing what they saw in the light of the flaming sky. Then both of them shrieked with horror at the scene below. "No! No! It can't be!"

They were cut off from the mainland.

Where once kilometers of rich vegetation had spread toward the Towers, the sea now reflected the blazing sky. It rose like a flaming mountain range with waves surging over its top flinging froth.

Then, abruptly, dramatically, the scene changed in this gone-mad world.

Howling hideously, water drained away to reveal endless kilometers of devastation. Savaged by the monster the sea had become, torn and bleeding fields fell away. A labyrinth of seething dark trenches replaced the green-and-gold cropland.

Continuing its dizzying retreat, the sea sucked away at the earth below them. Boulders tumbled like pebbles. The undermined mountain they stood on seemed about to crumble. At each side of them the snarling sea flung itself away to the north and south.

Then it returned, filling the abyss. Its towering, crimson-crested waves raged higher and higher.

Philip and Vita clung together saying comforting words to one another as they sat on a rock and watched all through what seemed a never-ending night.

Day came at last. The flames in the sky slowly faded to a red glow. The bubble of blood that was the moon passed overhead. But the sun's scorched coming relieved nothing. The upheaval continued. Land dissolved before their eyes. Hour after hour the mountains of water surged and ebbed. The shoreline beyond became more distant.

Philip and Vita surveyed the changes as their mountain became an island far, far out to sea. Often Vita peered down toward the aerotrailer, while, again and again, Philip turned toward the Towers.

Once he looked to the south and pointed. "See that, Vita? There's another island."

Vita nodded. "Not big like this one."

Philip wondered briefly if there were survivors on that island.

As the day wore on, the sun remained a dead red ball

crossing a copper sky, but the shaking subsided. Philip grew hot and sleepy. He was hungry and thirsty, too.

Wearily, disregarding the danger, he grasped Vita's hand to pull her to her feet. "Let's go see if the aerotrailer is still there."

The long, winding way they'd taken to the top of the mountain had become a huge rockslide that engulfed all but the front of the aerotrailer.

Slowly, Philip picked his way over the rocks. Tired as he was, the little aerotrailer, a copy of his home in the Towers, drew him. He ached for his bed, food, and water.

Ahead of him Vita walked almost as slowly. Now and then, shielding her eyes from the glare, she gazed anxiously across the cactus-covered mountainside as if examining each clump of bushes.

As they approached the aerotrailer, Philip pointed at a crazy chewed-up pile of sticks. "Can you believe it? That's what's left of our picnic table and benches."

Vita said, "And look at our door." A heap of crystals was all that remained of the tempered glass door.

The aerotrailer itself appeared undamaged. It lay there, half covered in its nest of rocks like a large silver egg. On top, the seawater converter was just as his father had left it, with their plastic jugs tied to it.

A pile of rocks blocked their entrance and gravel rattled down as Vita climbed over it to go inside to the kitchen. When he followed across the tilted floor, she blocked his way. Arms flung out in a gesture of hopelessness, she cried, "It is ruined! Everything is ruined! Oh, Philip, what will we do?"

Philip looked. "It's a real disaster area!" he said glumly.

Aside from its angle, the room seemed okay, but the doors

to the refrigerator, freezer, and cupboards hung open. Their contents covered the floor. Even the insta-machine was smashed, its plastic bubble ajar.

Philip picked his way along the slope past the refrigerator to the freezer that held his insta-meals. Shelves on its door, as well as inside, oozed melting insta-meals in glutinous masses.

With his thumb and forefinger, Philip picked one up. Its label, "insta-chick" dangled from it. He showed it to Vita. "Yuck!" he said. "I can't eat that." Once he'd tried eating a defrosted insta-meal. It had been like chewing rubber bands.

Vita crouched to search through the assortment of food in front of the refrigerator. She picked over the supplies Philip's father had stored there for her. He watched her place the vegetables on the counter. Then he saw her yellow cheese, and his mouth watered. He told her "Nothing is the world would taste as good as a piece of that cheese!"

He reached for it, but Vita pushed his hand away. "Wait until I fix it for you." She laid the cheese on the counter with the vegetables and stooped to pick up a package of wafer-thin corn cakes.

He watched, surprised, as she reached under her plaid shirt to reveal what appeared to be a concealed weapon, forbidden to the Tower people. From a leather sheath on her belt she drew a shining knife, with which she began busily shredding cheese, tomatoes, and lettuce onto a corn cake.

When she folded it up and handed it to him, Philip laughed weakly. "That looks like a great sandwich! Thanks!" He took a bite and gazed admiringly at Vita. He'd eaten many similar sandwiches in his insta-meals, but he'd never before seen one made.

He gobbled it down. Then he picked up one of the plastic

glasses from the floor and filled it with water at the sink under the water tank.

With her sandwich in her hand, Vita drew a glassful, too.

When they had finished, Philip started to refill his glass, but Vita stopped him. She pointed to the dial that indicated the number of liters in the transparent tank. "Water is precious."

Philip stared at the dial and then at her. "I know how to work the desalter. Don't worry about it."

But he didn't drink any more water. Maybe the desalter had been smashed. And if it hadn't been smashed, could he run it? His father had told him how it worked. But would he remember? He tried to think of his father's instructions, but he was too tired.

He put his glass down. "I'm going to bed," he told Vita. He had just taken a step toward the back room when the aerotrailer shook violently. Philip ran toward Vita. Suddenly he could cry. Hot tears burst from his eyes. "This is too much! Won't it ever end?"

She didn't answer.

Through the blur of his tears, Philip saw that she was gulping, trying to swallow the tears she, too, had held back for so long. Her wiry body trembled and swayed with the sound of deep, convulsive sobs.

Philip wanted to comfort her. He hadn't meant to like her, but he couldn't seem to help himself. "Vita," he pleaded, "don't cry, Vita. Please don't cry. It can't go on forever."

5
Bread to Live

The next morning Philip awakened to what he thought might be rain on the roof. But almost at once he realized that the drumming was far louder than rain could ever be. Rocks clattered down as the aerotrailer gently settled into place following another aftershock.

In almost total darkness, Philip leaped out of bed, fumbling for his shoes and socks. As he put them on, the rocks slowly stopped falling. His mind began to play back the earthquake that had left him and Vita alone on this island, his worry about his parents, and the problems he and Vita faced without Central Power. He remembered the blazing sky and blast when Central Power blew up and shuddered to think of it.

But now he felt the rumble in his own stomach. He was starving, and he thought of the good cheese in the sandwich Vita had made for him the night before. He'd watched her and thought he could make his own.

He got up and, automatically, flipped the light switch. Nothing. Of course not. But why was it still dark? Philip listened to the comfortable robot voice of his watch: "The time is exactly ten three and forty-five seconds" and studied his room's little window. Of course. It was dark because the aerotrailer was half buried in the rockslide.

He ran out to make his sandwich, and in the dim light

nearly stumbled over Vita. She knelt on the sloping floor in front of the cupboard, carefully scooping up the heap of whitish stuff that lay there.

Her sober eyes stopped him. In a reverent voice, she explained, "This is flour to make corn cakes... bread. We need bread to live. If we do not have flour..." her voice fell away.

Philip gazed down on her. Suddenly she was a stranger again. A scrawny, oddly dressed stranger who groveled on the floor babbling about flour. Philip hardly knew what flour was. He didn't quite know what parts of his insta-meals had been made of flour.

But he was hungry. Where were the corn cakes and cheese? The doors of the refrigerator and freezer still hung open. The insta-machine had been returned to the counter, but there was no food in sight.

Vita glanced up at him. "If you are looking for breakfast, there is none."

He couldn't believe her. "But the corn cakes... the cheese!"

She nodded her head toward the broken-out door. "The animals came. They ate the food." She shrugged. "You and I will pick up the flour. Then you make a fire. I will cook the corn cakes."

Philip gulped. No food! Make a fire? He couldn't believe it. Did she really think he could make a fire? Stunned, he knelt down beside her to help her pinch up the last of the powdery flour and add it to the contents of the plastic bowl she was holding. For today, anyway, he'd take orders from her even though she came from the Open Country and couldn't know much. His people, the survivors of the acid smog who established the technology of the self-sustaining Towers, were smart; Vita's people had been stupid to live with nature. That's why they had starved to death. Still, he had no choice but to do what she said until Central Power was fixed.

As they worked, he asked Vita about the animals. "I tried to feed popcorn to a raccoon, an opossum, and a skunk just before the quake. But they wouldn't eat it. Wasn't that weird? And I've been wondering which animals ate the yellow cheese. Did you see them?" he asked.

"See what?"

Philip looked at her closely. Why was she acting so dense? Yesterday during all their trouble she had seemed such a nice person. "Did you see the animals?"

"Oh, yes. I saw them."

"Which ones?" Philip wondered if Oscar, the tame rabbit, had come to join the feast.

"Well, I scared off a raccoon," Vita said.

Philip looked at the floor in front of the refrigerator for tracks or scraps. "Did you clean up?"

Her voice was cross. "Of course. Now, come on, I will help you make a fire pit for your fire."

When they stood up, Philip saw that the matches had tumbled off the shelf. He picked them up and showed them to Vita. "How am I supposed to know how to make a fire? With Central Power so easy to tune in, who needed a fire?"

Together they heaved aside a few rocks blocking the doorway and climbed over the rest.

Vita pointed to the splintered picnic table and benches. "That will burn just fine."

Philip carried some of the wood to a sandy spot Vita chose.

It was next to the rockslide and as close as possible to the aerotrailer. There she began to scoop out a hole.

When Philip understood what she was doing, he helped her dig and then line the hole with stones.

At the back of the pit, Vita tilted a flat rock, and told Philip, "Go scout around for dry grass and leaves." When he returned with them, she showed him how to place the wood, then where to touch the match.

He lit the fire carefully, shielding the flame with his hand, and was rewarded by the crackling blaze that sprang up.

But for the first time, he really began to worry about the future. What if his parents didn't come back right away? Would every hot meal mean building a fire like this? If so, they would soon run out of matches. Philip sat on a rock by the fire and counted them. Forty-nine were left in the box.

When Vita returned, she carried a bowl full of a whitish mixture. He watched her in amazement as she expertly slapped a ball of the mix from hand to hand until it flattened into a thin disk.

"What's in the bowl?" Philip asked.

Vita spared him a glance. "Why, dough, of course."

"Yeah? What's it made of?"

"Just corn flour and water. It is the way I shape them that makes the corn cakes." She slowed her slapping to show Philip how she did it. "Someday I will teach you."

Philip couldn't believe he would need to learn how to make his own corn cakes. Soon help would come. He'd be back to eating insta-meals. To change the subject, he asked her, "Is the fire okay?"

Vita smiled and nodded, kicked the now hot backup stone into place over the coals, and laid the flat round of dough on it.

The smell was tantalizing. Philip drew in a deep breath.

While that corn cake baked, Vita formed another. As soon as the first one had cooled enough, Philip ate it. But when he reached for the next one, Vita stopped him. "It is my turn."

He nodded. His mother would have called him greedy. "I'm sorry," he said.

When they'd eaten two corn cakes apiece, Vita patted out dough to bake more of them on the hot stone. Soon she had a pancakelike stack, and had emptied her bowl of dough.

Philip sat on his rock by the fire pit and watched. "Are those for our dinner?" he asked. He thought of the raccoon eating the package of corn cakes spilled in front of the refrigerator last night. They had been sealed in a plastic bag, and Philip remembered how Vita had carefully tied it after taking out what they needed. It had been nearly full. The raccoon must have been very hungry. And the vegetables— some tomatoes and lettuce that she hadn't used. What had happened to them? And, of course, that delicious yellow cheese. Even with his stomach filled with hot corn cakes, he wished he had some of that good cheese.

Vita piled her stack of corn cakes in the empty bowl. "For dinner we will have these and some beans. I will show you." She began to climb over the rocks that hid the aerotrailer from view. Her long blond braid swung over her red plaid shirt.

Philip spoke to her back. "Didn't that raccoon eat an awful lot of food?"

Suddenly Vita seemed to think that he had challenged her. Glancing back, her eyes turned to stone and her chin lifted. She snapped, "Are you suggesting I lied to you?" She flipped her braid and hurried on without waiting for an answer.

Philip told himself that he didn't care. But he really did care. He wanted Vita's eyes to smile at him and her voice to soften. He wanted her to understand that it was possible for him to be an equal even though he was younger than she was. Couldn't he ask a perfectly sensible question without making her mad?

6
Water Is Precious

Would she lie to him? Philip wondered. He'd heard the Open Country people did strange things when they were starving. Could she be hoarding food? He remained sitting by the fire after Vita passed from sight over the part of the rockslide that hid the trailer.

He wished he could talk to his parents. Every minute he ached for their return, but now he also needed them in a different way. He wanted to ask them about the little animals they had studied. How he wished he'd eaten his insta-meals with his mom and dad! Then he'd at least know what they had fed the little animals, how much, and what kind of food they ate.

But why was he questioning Vita? She was the one who knew how to make corn cakes. She did all the work. What reason did she have to lie?

Suddenly he remembered his own work. After he had checked out Central Power, they would have the arduous task of hauling water for the desalter. He ran over the rocks to the aerotrailer.

First, he turned into the kitchen to get a drink. Vita was on a high stool, stretching to reach inside the top cupboard. "What are you doing?" Philip asked.

Vita slammed the cupboard closed as if she hadn't wanted him to see. Then she flung it open and withdrew a cloth-wrapped bundle to show him. "My corn cakes. I am hiding them from the animals."

"Good!" he said. He turned his back and drank a glass of water while she climbed down. At the same time he glanced at the dial to see how much water remained in the tank. "We've got a little more than twelve liters," he told Vita. "But that's not a lot. I'll bring down the jugs from the roof. You'll help me haul water, won't you?"

Going to the beach with his parents had always been a frightening experience for Philip. Now he had to go there without them. He turned around to face Vita and saw that she, too, looked afraid. Her eyes were wide with alarm. "No, no! The big waves might come again. Earthquakes can cause tidal waves! I thought you knew. You told me the earthquake was coming."

Philip nodded. It seemed a long time ago that he'd read on the telescreen about the animals' forecasting the earthquake. He told Vita about the printout, and about the strange behavior of the raccoon, skunk, and opossum, as well as the rabbit.

When Vita heard about the rabbit, she fixed her eyes on Philip in a conspiratorial way. "He is good to eat," she said.

Philip stared at her. Had he heard her right? Would she eat Oscar? All kinds of rumors had circulated in the Towers about what the Open Country people were forced to eat when they were starving. Some people said they even ate one another!

He planned ahead as to what he would do when they took

the trail to the beach. Before they came to the bushes, he would talk, or shout, or whistle. Anything to scare Oscar away.

But now he wanted to know about the tidal wave. "Are you talking about the kind of wave that cut us off from the mainland?"

Vita nodded. "Something like that. They are called tsunami waves. Earthquakes in the ocean cause them."

"Whew!" Philip breathed. He thought the waves he'd seen on the beach were threatening enough. No way did he want to risk coming close to anything larger.

But the problem was water. Just one shower took about six liters. "What are we going to do about filling the tank?"

"If we are careful, there is enough. It is for drinking and cooking only." She glanced down the little hall. "We do not need the bathroom."

Philip almost said, Maybe you don't, but I do. Then he thought about it. The chemical toilet didn't use water. Without his mother there to remind him, he'd skipped his shower. All he really used water for was to clean his teeth and slick down his bushy hair. "I'll be careful," he told Vita.

"We have another problem," she said. "There is not a lot of firewood until we can bring up driftwood from the beach. We need wood to cook the beans." She lifted the lid off the cooking pot on the counter, and Philip peered in.

"Will that be enough for us?" he asked. There was only a layer of red beans in the bottom of the pot, which was full of water.

Vita smiled. "They will swell up to fill it. You will see."

He followed her outside to the fire pit, where she used a green limb to prod the hot stones, rearranging them so that the pot of beans was buried in hot coals with the stones and fire on top.

"They will cook all day," she told him.

She began to tear the few nearby scattered limbs into a size small enough to burn, and Philip copied her. When he had stacked them conveniently by their fire pit, he saw that there on the stone where he'd left it was the precious box of matches.

He scolded himself, took the matches inside, and put them on the cupboard shelf alongside the first-aid kit. Then he checked out Central Power by turning the switches on the telewall on and off. Nothing happened. Somehow he'd known it wouldn't. Maybe tomorrow, he told himself.

He was pretty sure the telewall receiver hadn't been damaged. He seemed to remember that its parts were unbreakable.

He hoped the seawater converter had been made the same way. He climbed up on the roof of the aerotrailer to look at it, on the way tossing aside enough rocks to let light in his window. But there was no way to tell. Until he poured the seawater into the catalytic solar tank and heard the faint grinding sound of that wonderful chemical, Jonesite, magnetizing salt, he wouldn't know if it really worked.

The plastic solar panels that ran the length of the trailer appeared undamaged. However, to heat water, the buried end over the bathroom would have to be uncovered to receive the sun's rays.

The six plastic four-liter jugs he and his parents used were waiting, so he untied them and gathered them up by their handles, three in each hand. He walked the long way around, circling up over the gravel and rocks that covered the back end of the aerotrailer. He wanted to study the mountainside where the cactus grew. That's where the little animals live, Philip told himself. I wonder what they eat up there.

All at once the slide began to move. Rocks clattered. Philip found himself and his six jugs toppling. Bumping and tumbling, jugs around him, he rolled down almost to the front door of the aerotrailer.

Vita ran to help him. "Philip! Philip! Are you all right?"

Shaking inwardly, he jumped up and brushed himself off. "S-sure. Y-yes. Of course." What more could happen?

Vita bent to examine his left knee. "You are bleeding. Come on inside."

She led him to the cupboard, took down the first-aid kit and pointed to the tubes of medications. "Which kind do you choose?"

Coach's favorite insta-heal wasn't there so Philip said, "This one will do." He sponged off his knee and covered it with salve.

The unguent stung, and Philip couldn't keep his face from twisting.

He looked up to see that Vita's eyes had softened. "Too bad," she said. Then, as if to soothe him, she asked, "Shall we go see how big the waves are?"

Philip shrugged. "If you want to."

But as they walked along the bluff above the sea, his knee hurt. Again his soccer uniform made him sweat, and he remembered his mother's advice. Next time he'd wear his swim trunks. He was much too hot.

When he and Vita reached the point where they could see the longest sweep of beach, Philip realized that he was burning from more than heat. He'd forgotten to smear himself with sun screen. The skin on the exposed parts of his body seemed on fire. He was grateful when, high as they were above the sea, a wild wave now and then flung sparkling droplets on them. It felt good.

The high waves still frightened him, but he explained to Vita, "My dad and mom told me the waves were great. But I couldn't see it. I do now. Look at that blue! Did you ever see anything like it?"

She smiled. "I love the ocean."

Looking down from this height, Philip wondered why he'd found the surf so terrifying. These waves kept to a uniform pattern. The sea seemed very different—almost tame. Nothing like the wild fury that had cut them off from the mainland.

Yet the beach bore evidence that not long ago this sea had been on a rampage. Uprooted trees, as well as many objects too distant to identify, littered the shimmering sand.

When they started back, lunchtime was long past, and Philip's stomach started to rumble. He complained to Vita. "We should have brought a sandwich."

Her look questioned him. "But you had breakfast, and we will have beans for dinner."

"I meant for lunch," Philip said. "Don't you eat lunch?"

Vita shook her head and said firmly, "Two meals are enough."

For you, maybe, he thought. But he didn't argue. Vita came from a land of famine where people didn't have enough to eat. But that hadn't hurt her appearance. Now that he was used to her clothes, she didn't look very different from the Tower girls—especially Ariel, who certainly wasn't fat.

He admired Vita's surefooted grace as he followed her along the top of the bluff. They looked down at the ocean and talked over when they should risk filling their water jugs. Vita nodded over her shoulder at him as she weighed the question. "I think two days after the last aftershock will be safe."

Now they came in view of their fire pit, marked in the distance by faint heat-wave distortions. On its right lay the giant rockslide. On its left spread the cactus-covered mountainside dotted with three clumps of bushes.

As they walked, Philip looked closely, searching for the little animals. Suddenly he sensed that Vita, ahead of him, had tensed.

"What's the matter?" he asked. "Did you see something?"

Vita shook her head, but she started to walk faster. When they reached the fire pit, she eyed it sharply, then quickly knelt to push aside the hot rocks, lift the lid and peer into the bean pot.

As Philip watched, the fragrant aroma-laden steam reached his nostrils. "Oh, Vita!" he cried. "They smell wonderful! I want some!" The pot was half full—not full as Vita had said it would be. But there was plenty, he thought, for more than one meal.

"Wait!" Vita replaced the pot and jumped up. Her eyes looked worried although she smiled reassuringly. She ran over the rock pile, and Philip followed her into the aerotrailer's kitchen. With a glance at the water tank, she climbed onto the stool.

As he stopped to cool himself with a glass of water, he heard her sigh with relief. But when he read the water gauge, it said a little less than eleven liters. More than one liter had disappeared!

Before he could be sure he'd read it right, Vita grasped his arm. "Philip, come on outside." She was holding her bundle of corn cakes and smiling warmly at him. "I will show you how to make a bean sandwich."

"But Vita," he protested.

She didn't seem to hear and his stomach forced him to go with her. Maybe he'd misread the gauge that morning, and the thought of beans wrapped in a corn cake was too much for him to resist.

Possibly his sandwich wasn't as good as his insta-meal sandwiches, but because of his empty stomach, it tasted far better. He ate slowly, enjoying it, before he began to worry.

How could animals have eaten all that food last night? And what about the way Vita acted this afternoon? Had she seen something—or someone—as they came back from the bluff? She had seemed worried about the beans and, he thought, had been close to panic when she climbed onto the stool to make sure the corn cakes were safe.

Was she keeping something from him—trying to protect him? He thought of her round, troubled eyes and the way she had been rushing him around so he didn't have time to make sense of the dial on the water tank.

His mind flashed to the Scorpions. His father said they killed starving people. Well, he and Vita weren't starving now, but they might be soon. Could a Scorpion be hiding out there on the mountainside? Philip gazed up at the slope. Its muted colors, rising against the deep-blue sky, appeared as tranquil as ever. Yet who could tell?

Again Philip felt like wrapping his head with his arms, just as on the day when he first came here. Why had they come? It had been a terrible mistake. He didn't allow himself to imagine what the quake had done to the Towers. Instead he thought about the aerotrailer. It was no longer a refuge. Without Central Power, there was no climate control, and without a door, anything or anyone could come in.

Just as he'd known, it was dangerous out in the open. The sun had burned his skin. His legs were on fire between his socks and his shorts, and his face blazed. Why hadn't he followed his mother's pattern and used sun screen? Was it too late now?

Suddenly he thought of the burn ointment in the first aid kit. He rushed inside, opened the cupboard, and found the salve. While he spread it over his legs and face, he noticed that the match box had been moved a few centimeters. Had Vita moved it?

Hastily he rubbed the last of the unguent into his hands and opened the matchbox.

Some of the matches were gone. He counted. There were only thirty-nine instead of the forty-nine he'd counted that morning. This time he was certain.

Let Vita try to blame the animals for that!

7
The Hungry Boy

Philip charged out to the fire pit. He waved the box of matches under Vita's nose and shouted, "Someone took ten of our matches! Look!"

Vita backed away from him, her eyes troubled, her voice low. "Yes, I know."

Philip didn't care if his voice was harsh and angry. "Who did it?"

Vita gulped. "A boy. A boy who came on the aerobus with me. But I did not know he would steal. He is an orphan. His parents died in the famine."

Philip frowned. Could he believe her? "A boy? What kind of a boy? An Open Country boy? A Scorpion boy?"

"Oh, never!" Vita cried. "Not a Scorpion! The Scorpions kill people. This is just an Open Country boy who steals matches to light his fire."

Philip glared at her. "Are you kidding? That guy is a rat! He robbed us of all the food we had, vegetables, corn cakes! And that good cheese!"

Vita's eyes avoided his. "That is true," she said softly. "But on the aerobus he told me that he was hungry, very, very hungry." She lifted her chin and looked at Philip in a but-you-wouldn't-understand way. "Philip, you just cannot possibly know how it is," she said in a low, intense voice. "You have never been hungry. I mean really hungry."

He stamped his foot and swore. "I'm hungry right now. Really hungry! And this rotten kid is stealing my food!"

Vita looked at him sadly. "Believe me, I did not know . . ."

Philip interrupted. "How old is he?" Had Vita brought her boyfriend? The thought that she might have one had crossed his mind, but now he felt he couldn't bear it. He felt relieved when Vita shrugged and said, "About as old as you."

Her eyes pleaded with him. "I would have asked your parents. But they are not here."

Philip wondered about that. His parents had gone to meet Vita at the border, and she had come on the aerobus. But he'd worry about that later.

Vita went on. "He is without a name—a no name. In my country there are many girls and boys without names." She sank down onto a stone across the fire pit from Philip.

He spoke impatiently. "Well, where is he now?"

Vita nodded toward the mountainside. "Maybe there. I do not know. No Name lives anywhere."

"Up there? But there are no houses."

"He is a wild boy. He needs no house."

"But, Vita . . . where does this No Name sleep?"

She smiled at him as if he weren't too bright. "On the ground, of course."

Philip couldn't believe it. "Out in the open?" He turned his head to look at the sky reddening toward sunset and at the cactus-covered mountain. "No Name lives out there with the animals?"

Vita nodded.

"But how does he do it?" He thought for a second and his anger returned. "Don't tell me. I know. This No Name is a dirty, rotten thief."

Vita looked at him as if he'd stabbed her. "Oh, no! Do not call him that! He is just hungry."

"I'm hungry, too. I think he should ask if he wants to share. Not steal."

Vita's head dropped. "I will tell him."

To himself Philip repeated her words: I will tell him. What was going on? Had Vita been seeing this rotten No Name behind his back? Had she been helping him steal? The horrible memory of that night on top of the mountain when his whole world fell apart flashed through his mind. He had believed in her. Trusted her. She was his friend and more. Or he'd thought she was.

But what could he do? Until his parents came back, he had no choice. He would have nothing at all to eat if Vita didn't know how to make corn cakes and beans. He held his talking watch to his ear, then looked at the date on its face. It was now almost twenty-four hours since he'd last seen his parents. That would have been a very long time to go without food. He remembered his last insta-meal with its crispy chicken and strips of fresh pineapple. His mouth watered. How awful to have nothing else to eat but corn cakes and beans.

Then he thought of No Name and the famine in the Open Country. Perhaps, like him, No Name was grateful for anything at all to eat. But the good yellow cheese still bothered Philip. No Name had taken more than his share. What kind of person was he? Curiosity took control of Philip. He had to see No Name, find out what this "wild boy" looked like. He'd tell him not to steal their food, or he'd knock his block off. But a wild boy from the Open Country probably wouldn't understand English. And he might be big.

Then Philip remembered the water. This kid had stolen more than a liter. And no one but Philip knew how to run the desalter to make fresh water. But did he remember? Well, he could brag a little, pretend he did.

He told Vita, "When you see No Name, invite him to breakfast."

She laughed, jumped up, and bent slightly to throw her arms around him. "Oh, Philip! Philip! You are so kind!"

Philip found himself hugging her in return. He pretended this was an everyday affair—hugging a girl. But it felt so good, his thinking blurred. He managed to mumble, "I just want to see what this kid, No Name, looks like."

8

The Arrival of No Name

Philip had built the fire and watched Vita shape and bake his corn cake and fill it with beans. There was no No Name in sight. He'd finished eating his first sandwich before he asked about him.

Vita shrugged. "He will come." With her knife she turned the corn cake she was baking for herself on the hot stone.

Philip watched the mountain slope above him. After a while he saw a short, muscular boy come running, scrambling, sliding through the thorny bushes and cactus. He crash-landed by the fire pit, hand thrust out for food, head thrown back. Arrogant. He sat there cross-legged, hair dirty and uncombed, pants faded rags. But his bold black eyes challenged Philip.

Philip had never seen anything like him. He could hardly believe he was real. Turning to Vita, he whispered behind his hand, "Does he speak English?"

She looked doubtful. "The wild boys speak the Open Country language." Then she held thumb and forefinger a tiny space apart. "Try him."

Philip spoke cautiously but firmly to the black bullet eyes. "*Yi*. My name is Philip. What is yours?"

But there was no response until Vita placed a rolled-up corn cake in the outstretched hand. In seconds it was devoured, and No Name's tongue was unleashed.

His response was bewildering. The high troubled voice

mixed the strange Open Country language with English and went on and on. Philip could understand only a few words. "No Name" and "hungry" were among them.

Philip decided to ask Vita later about what No Name had said, but right now there was one worrisome question he had to ask. "No Name, where were you during the earthquake?" Philip shook himself to make his meaning clear. During that terrifying night, had this kid been here all alone?

No Name copied the way Philip shook, turned and pointed up the mountainside. "I scared. I hide." He waved a red-stained finger at the aerotrailer. "Is no one."

Vita's eyes narrowed as she watched No Name's red hands. She laid another piece of wood on the fire before she spoke. "I do not think No Name was that hungry. He has eaten the cactus fruit. I think No Name likes to eat." Her eyes searched the wild boy up and down. Then suddenly she lunged at him. Her hand dug what was left of the yellow cheese from his pocket. "Sssso!" she hissed into his face. "You said it was all gone. Not only are you the thief; you lie, too!" She pointed back toward the mountainside. "Go! Get out of here! We do not feed the liar and thief."

No Name's lower lip pushed out like a baby's. He fell to his knees. Huge tears burst from his eyes. "Please! Please!" he pleaded in a stream of words Philip couldn't understand.

Philip tried to speak, but Vita stopped him.

Again she pointed, her soft eyes turned to gray stones, her voice unrelenting. "No Name! Go!"

Reluctantly No Name slumped toward the mountain. But, just out of Vita's reach, he turned and rested on his haunches to watch them.

As if No Name weren't there, Vita calmly patted out a corn

cake and laid it on the hot rock. Then, pulling the knife from the sheath on her belt, she turned it. The blade flashed as she shredded cheese onto the corn cake. The cheese bubbled temptingly, each popping bubble bombarding Philip's nose. When he cupped his hands to receive the delicious treat, he bent his head over it. Moving the hot corn cake from hand to hand, he waited for it to cool. His nose moved back and forth with it, delighting in the smell. He could see that No Name, too, was drinking it in. Then his shoulders slumped, and he took off up around the mountain.

Good enough for him, Philip thought, as he sat back to enjoy his corn cake and cheese. He ate slowly and tried not to think of what No Name's coming might mean.

9 He Hates Me

When he had finished his corn cake, Philip looked up at the mountainside where No Name had disappeared. He pulled his earlobe. Of course he didn't want anything really bad to happen to No Name, but he wished he'd go back where he came from. Why had Vita brought him, anyway?

After a while he got up. He had other things to do. His sunburn hurt, and the sun was already hot. He'd rub some more salve on the burned parts, then take off his shirt and cover himself with sun screen. The very thought of his mother rubbing on the sun screen overwhelmed him. Where are you, Mom and Dad? Why don't you come back?

His eyes searched the sky for the stream of aerotraffic.

Nothing but the endless blue. Since the quake, every high-flying gull brought a flutter to his heart—a hope that the world was becoming normal again.

He ran into the little kitchen to get the salve in the first-aid kit. As he rubbed it on, he caught sight of his still flaming face in the refrigerator's mirroring door. His freckles seemed to jump out of his sunburn. His usually flat-combed brown hair stood straight up. And his endurocloth soccer suit's vivid colors were dimmed with dirt.

No wonder No Name hadn't liked him much. Who would?

He ran to his room, brushed his hair, and changed from his soccer clothes into his swim trunks. And to keep organized, as his soccer coach had told the team they should, Philip folded his blue-and-gold-striped soccer shirt and laid the blue shorts on top of it. Just to be doing what he and his friends had done together over and over reassured him, made him believe that sometime he'd be back with his parents and friends again.

After he and Vita had cleaned up the trailer and stacked all the wood from the picnic table and benches by the fire pit, they again made the trip to check on the beach.

Today the sea seemed calmer. The last quake had been yesterday at about ten o'clock.

Vita told him. "Maybe tomorrow afternoon it will be safe to bring up some water. I hope so."

"So do I," Philip said. "No Name drank more than a liter yesterday."

She shrugged. "You say you can run the seawater desalter. Why should you worry if a thirsty boy takes a drink?"

Philip felt annoyed, then angry. Did Vita want this wild kid to help himself to anything at all that he wanted? He wondered what No Name was taking in their absence today. On the way home he asked Vita.

Her answer was cool. "We shall see."

But as they came within view of the fire pit and its shimmering gases, Philip saw that something lay beside it. They hurried to find out what it was.

Philip was surprised to see one of the stickery oval pads from the gray-green cactus that grew on the mountainside. On it lay a small heap of fuzzy, deep-red fruit.

Before Vita could stop him, Philip had picked one up. Immediately he squealed, dropped it and sucked his fingertips. He'd found that the fuzz was, in fact, cactus barbs.

Vita shook her head at him. "Grow up. Do not be in such a hurry." Then she pulled out her knife, stabbed one of the fruits, and tasted the red drops that clung to her knife. She offered the remaining droplets of juice to Philip. "It is like candy. You will love it."

In spite of his hurt fingers, he smiled when he tasted the sweet juice, and Vita, with a skilled hand, pared out the cactus spines and cut the fruit for him to eat. It was filled with hard seeds he had to spit out, but it tasted like the rich, red syrup of a berry insta-pie. She fixed him several others, all the time looking more and more worried.

"No Name is a good guy to bring these to us," Philip said. To please Vita he'd been trying to find something good to say about No Name.

But Vita scowled. She pushed the hot rocks aside and inspected the beans. "He has had some," she said.

She ran, with Philip following, to the sink. "He has had some water, too."

Then, on tiptoe, reaching from her stool, she pulled out

her hidden corn cakes. Her voice was triumphant. "No Name did not find them!"

"Good!" Philip said. But he wasn't sure there was anything to cheer about. Should he be glad just because No Name hadn't found something he would have wanted to steal?

Philip turned his back on Vita and strode into his room. Instantly he knew something was wrong. What was it? Was No Name hiding somewhere?

In the dim light he saw his soccer clothes. Instead of being neatly laid out as he had left them, they lay twisted into ugly lumps.

No Name had been there.

Philip picked up his shirt. No Name had tied it into tight knots. He studied the knots and pictured the anger in No Name's face when he twisted the tough blue-and-gold fabric.

No Name must really hate me, Philip thought. I wonder why? Well I hate him, too. Even if he isn't scared to live out there on the mountain all alone, and knows how to hunt and fish and find his own food. . . . Philip thought of the people he knew. Not even his hero, Bernard Finch, could do that.

Again, Philip looked at his knotted-up soccer clothes and in his mind's eye saw No Name and his muscular body. He was built like Bernard. He probably would have made a good soccer player.

But forget that, Philip told himself. Right now No Name had come between him and Vita. The warm feeling he'd had for her remained, but she treated him like a child and No Name as an equal.

I hate No Name, Philip told himself. I don't care if he hates me, too.

10 A Nest in the Cactus

Philip tried to think of a reason for No Name to hate him. What had he done?

But why should Philip feel guilty? What right had No Name to be here? Uninvited, he'd come with Vita. She had sneaked him in from the aerobus. Once again he wondered if it really had been a mix-up that Vita hadn't met his parents at the border.

But that was silly. Surely she hadn't brought this crazy kid all the way from the Open Country. Or had she? That was the only reason Philip could think of for deliberately missing his parents at the border.

Well, if she had to bring someone, why this thieving No Name, who seemed to think he owned her? Why couldn't she have brought someone like Bernard Finch or one of the other kids on his soccer team?

Philip tried to imagine how it would have been in the Open Country during the famine. The news had been full of horrors, and it all pointed to the foolishness of not using scientific methods to obtain water to grow their food. Vita said, "We need bread to live," that first day when they'd scooped up the spilled flour that made the corn cakes. And that was the truth. Now he understood. Food and its ownership meant the difference between life and death. No Name, who had stolen their food, could, if he stole in the Open Country, be a murderer.

Dirty, rotten guy, Philip thought.

Then, hearing Vita in the kitchen, he went out to show her his knotted-up clothes. "Look what No Name did!" he said.

She shook her head, and her gray eyes clouded. "No Name did that?" Then she tried to explain. "It may be because he has never had clothes like yours. He envies you."

"You mean No Name is jealous?" Philip scowled and pulled at a knot until he untied a sleeve. He'd never guessed that anyone would be jealous of him, but he knew how it felt. He'd been jealous of the kid in school that Ariel had asked to a party but, of course, there was no one here to envy. Certainly not No Name. Even if Vita did seem to prefer him. He could never be jealous of that lout. He told Vita, "I don't want No Name in my room. Tell him to keep out!"

Vita lifted her chin. "If I see him, I will tell him," she said stiffly. "Now it is time for us to eat."

Philip was starving. Hastily he unknotted his clothes, put them on, and followed Vita outside to the fire pit. He tried not to care that he'd hurt her feelings.

But that was before he tasted his food. It wasn't much, but it was delicious. He wolfed down two corn cakes filled with beans and some strips of green.

When Vita told him the green was cactus, he stared in disbelief. "Cactus?"

"It is the cactus No Name brought. I cut out the spines with my knife and cooked the pieces in the pot with the beans."

Philip pointed to the hillside. "Cactus like those?"

Vita nodded. "They are called *nopales*."

Even though daylight was fading, the joined oval pads of the cactus showed clearly. There were hundreds of them, the tops of some rimmed with the red, apple-shaped fruit No Name had brought them.

And, somewhere up there on that mountainside, No Name lived. He had no name and no home. Like a wild animal, he had to sleep outdoors in the open. As Philip's eyes scanned the mountain, two deer like the ones they had seen during the earthquake wandered into view on the horizon. After they had passed, a skulking form followed. It seemed too rangy for a wild dog. Philip watched with trepidation.

"Look, Vita. It's a wolf!"

"No. It is not a wolf. It is a coyote. He tries to catch the deer. But the deer know how to protect themselves." She darted her hands to demonstrate how the doe's hooves could act like hammers to repel the coyote's attack on herself and her fawn.

"But No Name! How can he fight the coyote?"

Vita looked troubled. But she shook her head. "He will manage okay. We need not worry about No Name."

Philip peered up the hill. Even if No Name did lie and steal, living out there with those wild animals was pretty rough.

That night, Philip had trouble falling asleep in his dark little room. Everywhere he imagined shining disks that turned into animals' eyes staring greedily at him. And the eyes didn't belong to the little animals he knew—the raccoon, opossum, or skunk. They were the eyes of the coyote.

At breakfast the next morning Philip watched anxiously for No Name to come sliding down the mountain. When he didn't come, he asked Vita. "Where is No Name?"

She shook her head. "I do not know."

Philip said, "Maybe we could take him a corn cake."

She smiled and pointed up the mountainside. "We can take him a corn cake and, on the way, pick cactus fruit."

Philip agreed and examined his pricked fingers. Only a faint feeling of yesterday's barb remained. Today he would be more careful and plan ahead. Before they started off, he armed himself with a kitchen knife.

When they reached the cactus, Philip took a plastic sack Vita had given him and, stepping warily around the plant, cut off fruit and caught it in the bag. Now and then he treated himself by piercing a fruit with his knife and licking off the sweet drops of red juice.

He watched Vita cut another carefully selected pad and store it in her bag with the cactus fruit. "Now it is time for us to find No Name," she said. She pointed to three clumps of bushes. "He lives in one of them. Let us try this one." She called to No Name and easily picked her way among the stickery cactus and other thorny bushes.

Carefully, Philip followed in her footsteps.

It was in the third clump of bushes that they found No Name's ragged little blanket with his sweater rolled up beside it. They lay in a cushiony kind of nest made of seaweed grass. Blue-black seashells covered the ground, and nearby was a half-finished fire pit. What looked like dark-red paint splattered the stones.

Paint? It took Philip a moment to realize that it wasn't paint. It was blood!

He turned to Vita and saw that she had recognized the blood instantly. After peering anxiously in all directions, she cupped her hands to her mouth and shouted, "No Name! No Name!"

When No Name didn't come, Philip gazed at the blood again, gulped, and added his calls to Vita's.

11 Where Is No Name?

In time Vita turned to Philip. "I wonder where he could be."

"So do I," Philip said. The blood-spattered rocks were right there, but surely a coyote hadn't eaten all of him. There would be more than blood. He asked Vita, who bent to examine the ground near the rocks.

She pointed to animal tracks in the sand around the still moist seashells.

"No Name has been feeding the animals, I think." She turned over a few of the shells. Some of them had yellow flesh clinging to them. "No Name does not listen. I told him not to go to the beach. I warned him about the big waves." She looked anxiously toward the bluff. Again she called No Name. And again there was no reply.

Philip pointed to the bloody stones. "Is No Name hurt?"

Vita shrugged. "Maybe it is No Name's blood. Maybe it is an animal's."

Puzzled, Philip followed her as she hunted for No Name. She seemed to grow more and more angry as the day wore on. "When I find that No Name, I will fix him!"

As he plodded after her, Philip's worry increased. They walked all of the island's bluff, peering down at the beach and calling. Their voices were swallowed by the crashing surf. A dozen coves and seven or eight craggy outcroppings on the shore could have hidden him. They scanned the mountain over and over, then the rockslide. No sign of No Name.

Late in the afternoon, when they finally gave up their search, Philip's hunger pangs were so bad that he thought his backbone and stomach met. He looked forward to enough hot beans to fill him up, but they arrived to find their fire had gone out. Philip thought how stupid that was. If only they could plug in Central Power, they'd have no problems cooking their food.

He hurried inside to try the dials. Sitting on the bench in front of the screen, he worked them all.

Nothing. Nothing at all but the click of the switches.

His let his face fall into his hands. Mom! Dad! Where are you? His tumbling insides made him feel as if he were on a down elevator. Tears rose into his eyes. How could he live without his parents? They had to come back! They would come back! He pictured how it would be. Hugs and kisses. Everyone happy. Then his mother would say, "Let's eat," and the insta-meals would reconstitute, smelling delicious—this time with a steak for him.

Vita called, and when he joined her the tone of her voice sounded more apologetic than her words. "We spent too much time hunting No Name." Then she led him outside to the cold fire pit, where they ate a few cold beans wrapped in a corn cake, finishing with the cut-up fruits of the cactus.

For that and his cupful of water Philip was grateful. But he felt as if he'd only begun to eat. All of the strength seemed to have emptied from his arms and legs as they awaited food that didn't come. He felt weak and afloat in the unreal world.

Yet at sunset this unreal world glowed warmly. In the background the ocean orchestrated its own persistent crashing music, and somehow Philip felt that its offbeat rhythm blended better with his own body rhythms than the constant programmed music in Tower 117 ever had. He wondered about that. Now that he had spent a few days in this place, it seemed in some ways more homelike than the Towers. If only his parents were here and there were some way to get enough food. . . .

He glanced down at the seeds and skins of the cactus fruit he had left by the fire pit. Maybe Open Country people like Vita and No Name could live on this kind of stuff, but he needed more. Still, the cactus did provide food. In the fast-falling darkness he gazed at the mountainside covered with them.

What was that? A light! A tiny light! And it was near No Name's camp!

"Look!" Philip shouted. "Look!"

Although he knew no one was there but Vita, he wanted the whole world to know. No Name was safe! Wild animals hadn't killed him!

Vita grabbed his wrist and they ran, somehow dodging all the prickly cactus, toward the campfire.

On the way Philip's nose detected a new scent in the air. Instantly he knew what it was—the aroma of roasting meat. Oh, what a delicious smell!

Before they approached the circle of light around No Name, Vita pushed Philip back. Her eyes warned him, and she laid a finger over her lips.

Philip understood. It was her show. She led him to where they faced No Name's back.

Resting on his haunches, No Name watched his meat cook. It had been tied into a bundle with grass and was supported by forked branches. Philip's mouth watered as juices oozed from the meat to glimmer temptingly in the firelight.

He waited silently, wondering what Vita would do.

Suddenly, with no word of warning, she sprang between No Name and the campfire. In a quick burst of speech in Open Country language, she shot a question. Philip understood the meaning, if not all the words. "You took our food. Why do you not share yours?"

No Name turned so that Philip could see his face. As Vita scolded, Philip saw the boldness disappear from No Name's eyes. His hand swept under his shirt to slip out his knife. With it he cut down the roasted bundle of meat. On the rock beside the fire he carved a sure line, cracking right through the bones of the small animal. As the halves fell apart, he looked up at Vita.

After she'd nodded her satisfaction, she impaled half of the meat on her own knife, lifted it, and turned to go, nodding to Philip to follow.

Juices sloshed in Philip's mouth all the way down the hill to their own fire pit. Once there, Vita's knife flashed, glittering in the moonlight, as she carefully divided the meat into equal portions.

Philip pretended it was an insta-meal. He didn't want to think of the blood on the rocks and what it meant.

After he finished, Philip burped with his good feeling of fullness. He didn't know what he'd eaten: the rabbit, the raccoon, the opossum or the skunk. And he was never going to ask.

He just hoped it wasn't Oscar.

12 Without Vita

The next morning a shriek awakened Philip. It was Vita, and it came from the kitchen. What was wrong? He raced to help her and plunged into the welter of flying arms and legs—hers and No Name's.

Soon Philip found himself astride No Name, who was heaving with spasms of uncontrolled sobs.

Vita's words cut like her knife. From the Open Country words Philip had learned, he grasped what had happened. "...water...precious...you steal...the water is the life!"

No Name slumped and muttered what sounded like words of repentance. Then, even with both Vita's and Philip's weight on him, he managed to writhe in self-denunciation. His voice rose, and Philip understood that No Name was saying that, given another chance, he would die of thirst before stealing their water.

Vita, sitting on No Name's shoulders, peered back questioningly at Philip, who was astride his legs. She asked his opinion, "Do you think No Name is sorry enough?"

Philip nodded, and Vita's voice became conciliatory. "Do you like to be the wild boy? Do you always want to be the wild boy? Stealing...doing the bad thing?"

Pinned down as he was, No Name's body rose, thrusting them aside.

Vita and Philip scrambled to recapture him before he could escape. Vita shouted angrily while her hands busied themselves with his thick leather belt.

Philip pulled back. What was Vita doing? Taking away his clothes? He wanted No Name to go away and stop stealing their stuff. Without his clothes he couldn't go. He'd be forced to stay here.

But Vita slipped No Name's knife, enclosed in its sheath, off his belt and held it over his face in triumph. "Now what does the wild boy do?"

No Name spoke in his strange language, but Philip knew that he meant "nothing." That was true, Philip thought. Knives made all the difference.

Vita hadn't finished. "Without a knife you cannot be a wild boy. You will be like Philip."

No Name's hands rose in protest. Vita reached to help him up, and then returned his belt to him. As No Name looped his belt on, he eyed Philip coldly and shook his head. "I not be like him."

Vita scowled. "You will be like him, or . . ." she pointed up the mountain. "Or you will go without the knife." Then she lifted her chin, "If you go, you will not see Philip make the seawater into fresh water."

No Name stared at Philip in disbelief, then looked at Vita and half smiled. "No. He cannot do."

"Do not laugh," Vita said. "You think the wild boy knows it all. That is not true." She turned to Philip. "Tell him."

Philip fumbled. "If—if I-I can remember how it is done, I can do what Vita said—make the salt water fresh."

No Name lifted his chin. "I wait and see."

Haughtily, but now and then glancing at the watch on Philip's wrist, No Name helped Philip with the fire. Vita made corn cakes for them all. Then, laden with plastic containers, they picked their way down from the bluff to the beach. All signs of the trail Philip had traveled with his parents seemed to have tumbled away during the quakes. Only the clump of bushes where Oscar lived remained, and Philip remembered to sound a warning. He saw that in spite of the debris, the beach itself looked much the same.

Philip couldn't spare the time to inspect what had been washed ashore. Instead, he braved the charging waves, filled his containers, and hurried back up the trail with his mind full of questions. Was the converter going to work? Could he remember his father's instructions? Vita's explanation to No Name had made him sound like a magician. Could he deliver?

As they returned up the rocky bluff, No Name scrambled around Philip to make himself the leader of the procession. Philip heard the soft sound of Vita's footsteps following. Once there, all three of them climbed onto the roof of the aerotrailer.

Copying Philip, Vita and No Name dumped their seawater into the tank. Philip tossed rocks aside and tried to read the dials. His father had said to turn the one on the left slowly—he remembered that. But when he did it and waited for the faint clicking sound that told that salt was being magnetized, there was no sound. Then Philip remembered that he had really listened to the converter only once. Perhaps the noise came later when more salt had accumulated.

Philip, No Name, and Vita scrambled down off the roof. Standing by the sink, they waited for Vita to taste the water.

She drew a glassful, held it up to the light to show them the clarity, and swallowed deeply. Abruptly a surge of red suffused her face. Then, as if she could rid herself of the swallow, she braced herself and spat and spat into the little sink.

Before Philip ran to taste the water himself, he caught the

full impact of No Name's scornful stare. Then he watched, in dismay, as No Name took Vita's hand. Smiling up at her in an appealing way, No Name led Vita toward the doorway.

Holding her throat, Vita turned back to Philip. "I will go with"—gasp—"No Name." A fit of coughing overcame her. She gestured toward the mountain.

Philip's down-elevator feeling took over as he watched them leave. Was No Name taking Vita to his camp for keeps? Philip couldn't believe Vita would go and leave him. But why should she stay? What was there to keep her now that he'd failed to make the desalter work?

He turned on the faucet, caught a drop on his finger, licked it, and studied the gauge. It registered full. Full of what? Undrinkable seawater, which he knew had caused shipwrecked sailors to go mad. And how were they different from shipwreck survivors? Here they were on a waterless island. Philip felt certain that if there were fresh water anywhere, No Name would have found it. Wasn't that why he'd had to risk stealing their water?

The only reason for their surviving this long was because of the fresh water in the tank. And now it was gone. Why hadn't he had the sense to drain off the last few drops?

Philip slumped as he thought how foolish he'd been. Water, not food, was what the human body needed most. Without water he would shrink up like his insta-meals. He knew that the important thing the insta-machine's reconstituting did was add water.

He gulped. His mouth filled with saliva while his throat grew drier waiting for him to swallow. What was the best way to save the water in his mouth? Vita knew about these things. She had survived a famine.

He'd run after her and ask her. She couldn't just leave him

here to die. The least she could do, if she went up on the mountain to live with her thieving friend, was to teach him some of those skills that had saved her.

He ran outside.

Walking close together, Vita and No Name picked their way up the mountainside. Angrily Philip listened as their voices drifted down to him. He wished he knew what they were saying. If only he knew more of their strange language.

No Name repeated one word over and over. It wasn't believable to Philip, but it sounded as if he were saying the word for sister. Was No Name calling Vita "sister"? Philip thought scornfully, That's just what that rotten guy would do, make her believe he thought of her as a sister. He remembered that his mother had told him Vita would be like a big sister. She was that and a whole lot more. It was hard for Philip to accept that she had none of the warm feeling for him that he had for her—that she would leave him for No Name. How wrong he'd been!

Then he saw Vita reach under her shirt. She unbuckled No Name's knife from her belt and handed it back to him. No Name accepted it with a gracious nod.

So, Philip thought, now both of them have their own knives. With what they know from living through the drought and famine in the Open Country, they will be able to survive here in the wilds.

But what about me? What can I do?

13 Instructions

Vita's name rose up in Philip's throat. He wanted to call her—scream for her. But, remembering No Name's scornful look, he held back, trembling with the swallowed words. No way was he going to let No Name see his terror. Somehow, he'd get along. His parents would come back and rescue him. He'd make the connection to Central Power. He'd show that No Name!

But inside the aerotrailer, when he pushed the dials for Central Power, nothing happened. He raced out, climbed up onto the roof, and looked at the seawater converter. He felt like kicking it. Why hadn't it worked? The sun was passing overhead. Soon the opening for the solar rays would be in the shade.

He hurried back to the kitchen to drain the unprocessed salt water into the containers so he could start all over again. Making three trips, he lugged the jugs up onto the roof. In his haste to beat the sun, he spilled water over one of the dials. Rock dust washed off, trickling down the roof, spilling out of sight over the edge of the trailer. By the dial Philip saw the letters "*i-r-s-t*."

His mind exploded. How stupid he'd been! The directions were right there! He scrubbed his finger over the rest of the words. "Turn on first," it said.

He washed off the instructions on the rest of the dials. The sequence was so clear that any little kid could understand it. Then he remembered what his father had told him: the one dial on the left was hard to turn. It turned slowly.

Philip twisted the dials in their proper sequence, but, as before, he heard the water run through the filter into the tank. There was no clicking sound of salt being magnetized. Tears burst from his eyes. He tasted them when they ran down his face into his mouth. They were as salty as the seawater. He gulped and held the sweet, unsalted saliva that came into his mouth to save it. He sat still in the gravel on the aerotrailer's roof, pulled on his earlobe, and tried to think.

A cool breeze brushed his face. He looked down at the aperture for the solar rays. It was in the shade of the mountain. He shook his head. Of course! Why hadn't he paid attention to that? He would have to wait until tomorrow to test the directions on the dials. The sun had to shine into the opening.

Hope flooded through him. Again he climbed down to fill the containers and carry them up onto the roof. The first thing tomorrow he'd be up watching for the sun's rays to reach the opening. That is, if he lived until tomorrow. His mouth had less and less saliva in it. His throat felt as harsh and gravelly as the rock pile that nearly engulfed the aerotrailer.

Then Philip gazed up at the mountainside. The cactus fruit grew there. Each fruit held a few drops of thirst-quenching juice. And it was food. He was very hungry.

Stumbling down off the roof, he rummaged in a drawer to find the kitchen knife he'd taken the other time he and Vita gathered the fruit. But hunger drew his eyes to the top cupboard where Vita hid her corn cakes from No Name. He moved the stool, climbed up, and stretched to feel inside the shelf. They were there.

Then he heard someone coming and jerked his hand back. Vita was calling. "Philip!"

She rushed into the kitchen repeating his name before he could climb down. She looked up at him and her hands flew to her hips. "Sssso! No Name is not the only thief!"

"But, Vita! I didn't know you were coming back."

"Not coming back!" She shook her head at him. "Did you think I would leave you here all alone?"

Philip couldn't look at her. How could he have misjudged her so completely? She was his friend, and more. She did return his love! He climbed down and rushed to take her hands. "Vita, I'm sorry. I didn't mean to hurt your feelings."

She squeezed his hands. "You make me very sad."

He went on to explain, "You brought No Name here. I thought you were going to stay with him."

"Stay with No Name?" Vita looked puzzled. "He is the wild boy." She dropped his hands and pointed to herself. "I am not wild. I am like you." She smiled and turned away to hoist a bag up on the kitchen counter.

Cactus fruit and some thick, dark-green leaves spilled from it. "For now let us forget about all of our troubles and eat."

She wrapped the moist green leaves, which she called sea spinach, in corn cakes to eat out by the fire pit. Philip helped cut up the cactus fruit.

When they had finished, Vita gazed up at the dark side of the evening sky. Following a white star, a nearly round moon pushed up over the top of their mountain.

Vita seemed fascinated by it. She rose and pointed. "It is

the moon that brings the fish!" She nodded as if to congratulate herself. "The little fish called the grunion. You will see. Not tonight. It is the next nights. The moon will bring the fish."

Philip stared at her. He was overjoyed that Vita had come back to him. He loved her and his life depended on her. But had she gone mad? How could the moon bring fish?

14 "I Did It!"

The next morning, while Vita still slept, Philip sat by the seawater converter. He counted the hated freckles on his knees and slid his teeth over his dry lips. The wait for the sun to cast its rays into the solar aperture seemed endless.

When, at last, he felt sure that light had entered, he carefully turned the dials in the proper sequence, poured in the water, and listened.

A soft *click-click-click* began, slowly at first, then blending into the faint grinding sound Philip longed to hear. The wonderful machine was working!

Swiftly, Philip climbed down from the roof and ran into the kitchen. He rushed to turn on the faucet, filled the glass, and tipped it to his dry lips. The cool, fresh water was sweet in his mouth. He swallowed, and, absorbed in this newly recognized pleasure, drained glass after glass.

Then, cheering and shouting, he came back to the real world and ran into Vita's room. "Vita! Vita! It works! It works! I did it!"

When Vita had drunk as he had, they joined hands and danced, circling with joy. He'd saved them! He'd saved them! He, Philip, had done it!

After a time Vita said, "I will be right back!" She ran up the mountain to No Name's camp and returned with him chasing after her.

Without a glance at Philip, No Name grasped the plastic glass in his stained fingers, turned on the faucet, and drank and drank. Once he held the glass up to the window, allowing the light beaming through the water to multiply in moving patterns on the wall. Then he drank again.

At last he set the glass on the sink, cast a dull eye at Philip, and walked out the doorway. Without glancing back, he trudged slowly up the mountainside, the blackened soles of his feet seemingly impervious to the cactus. Holes in his faded pants fluttered with white threads. But his backbone was stiff and straight, and he held his shaggy head high in defiance.

Philip looked at Vita.

She shook her head. "It is too bad. He does not want to thank you." Then she stood tall. "But I will tell him. If he does not bring something for us to eat, he does not drink." She smiled. "He fishes and hunts." Then she turned back to Philip. "Let us fill the extra jugs."

While the desalter ground softly, they carried water from the ocean. Again and again they made the long climb down the bluff and up again to supply the tank and jugs with seawater.

At midday, Vita led the way along the beach to the rocks. "Now it is low tide, we will find food for dinner," she said.

Shrilling warnings, some sandpipers spread patterned

wings and tucked back their feet to lift off the shimmering sand. Others, much smaller and so quick-footed that Philip thought they looked motorized, dared each charging wave as they stabbed into the wet sand for food. As Philip and Vita strolled along, sleek gray-and-white gulls trundled out of their path.

Philip noticed that since early morning the beach had widened. Where cliff met sea, the black shells Vita called "mussels" glistened. Water caught in pools glimmered against dark stones.

Showered by spray, Philip held the plastic bag open to catch the blue-black mussels Vita hacked off the sides of the rocks with her knife. After a while her voice rose above the crashing waves to say, "That will be enough mussels." She took the bag and led him to a shallow tide pool.

Side by side, they peered into a lovely seaweedy world.

"Vita," Philip said. "Look at that! Look at all those things moving! I've never seen anything like it."

Tiny hermit crabs inhabiting lost small shells, crept among the flowerlike sea anemones—some green and some purple. Minute transparent fish zipped about. Creatures in silver and black turban-shaped shells left tracks on the sandy bottom. A red-brown rock moved and Philip saw it was a crab, but when he reached for it, his shadow fell across the pool, and it skidded sideways under a stone. He turned to ask Vita for help, and she caught one to show him how he could pick them up without getting his fingers pinched. She added other shelled creatures to the bag, including big purple-spined sea urchins, and Philip captured two crabs as large as small saucers, which he dropped in with the mussels.

At last, Vita slung the bag over her shoulder and led the

way back to the spot under the bluff where they could see the bushes where Oscar lived. This marked their makeshift trail.

Vita dropped the bag of shellfish there and turned to Philip. "Let us swim and get clean."

Using her toes, she slipped off her rubber sandals. In her halter top and shorts she waited for Philip to unlace his soccer shoes.

He looked down at his blue endurocloth shorts and saw that they too needed a swim.

Then he turned to face the ocean and was relieved to see that it looked far less threatening than it had when he'd come down with his parents. He couldn't let Vita know how afraid he'd been. She hadn't questioned whether or not he could swim. Philip knew kids who couldn't, but he'd had lessons in the pool at the Towers.

He felt good about that until he found that swimming in a pool at the Towers was not at all like swimming in the ocean. Before he knew what was happening, he felt himself swept under the blue-green water. He came up gasping and was immediately met by another wave.

Panicking, he looked for Vita, but salt water stung his eyes. The sea flung itself into his face and up his nose. Needles darted through his head bringing tears to his eyes.

Through the blur he saw Vita, tanned skin glistening, blond hair slicked back, circling, head up, around him like a sea animal. She laughed, teeth gleaming, as she reached out, touched him and turned, prepared to swim away.

Recognizing the game, Philip sniffed and blinked. He knew how to play! He'd been tagged, and forgetting to be scared, he dived into an oncoming wave and touched Vita.

Then, for as long as his breath lasted, he hid in the

green-glass wall of the next wave. When he saw her coming, he surfaced and dived again to evade her. In his best racing style he swam away.

Suddenly a huge wave roared over his head, and he felt himself being lifted and flung toward the beach. His left elbow crashed, grinding painfully into the sand. He crawled up onto the beach and tried to examine his arm. Turning it as far as he could, he watched his skin begin to ooze blood. It stung but also hurt more deeply. Maybe it was broken. Where was Vita? She would know.

At that moment Philip heard an unfamiliar sound in the sky. Looking up, he saw a strange, noisy little plane trailing black smoke. It was quite unlike the aerocars, aerobuses, or any of the other vehicles powered by Central Power. As it neared the beach, Philip could hear a voice coming from it, but it was still too far away to understand.

Philip forgot his injured arm and struggled back into the sea to hide. From the waves he watched the plane. He didn't know what to make of its black-and-silver marking in a strange geometric design.

A harsh voice commanded: "Attention, all ages! The Liberation Army needs you! Show yourselves to be counted for tomorrow's food drop." Then the message was repeated in the language of the Open Country.

Philip gasped. Suddenly the water chilled him, and he felt goose bumps rise on his skin. What had happened? Who was the person in that plane? And why didn't the plane show the North Continent's flag?

Then a terrible thought struck him, and he started to shake from head to foot. Could this be the paramilitary group—the Scorpions—that his father talked about?

15 Grunion

From the surf, Philip watched and trembled while the plane passed out of sight and hearing. Vita huddled beside him in the water, her eyes big and questioning. "Shall we do what he said?"

"No!" He grabbed her hand. "Come on! Let's hide!"

They scrambled to put on their shoes at the bottom of the bluff, and Vita shouldered the bag of shellfish before they tried to run up their barely visible trail.

Philip's terror increased when the path's loose gravel kept slipping away under his feet impeding his desperate scramble.

Before they even neared Oscar's bushes, Philip heard the distant roar of the plane returning.

Just in time, they dived into the bushes. Phlip felt himself shudder in response to the plane's rhythmic throb and heard the rough commands repeated.

Suddenly memory jolted him. Were they safe here where side by side they lay hidden? The scanner! This plane must have a scanner. Was there any use in hiding? He tried to remember what he knew about them. Their ability to detect a person depended on heat sensitivity. Together, his and Vita's bodies could form a hot spot. But separated, neither one of them was large. The sensor might overlook them or mistake them for an animal.

Hastily he explained to Vita. She looked frightened and

quickly moved away. They crouched, waiting as far from each other as the shelter of the bushes allowed.

"They could be Scorpions," he told Vita. "How do we know?"

"But, Philip, why would the Scorpions bring food?"

He shook his head. "I don't know."

Vita went on. "There's not much flour for corn cakes. We could use some flour."

Philip remembered her words: "We need bread to live." When she first said that, he hadn't understood what she meant. But now that he'd been hungry day after day, the meaning was clear. He thought of all his delicious insta-meals.

Food! How he'd love to have some real food. But could they trust that plane and its strange markings? He asked Vita, "What was that sign on the plane? Did you ever see it before?"

She nodded. "It is called a gammadion." She shook her head. "I do not remember what it means."

Philip sighed. "If only it were this country's flag."

Vita nodded. Then she said, "I think we will hide."

Because of its pattern of circling, Philip felt sure it was a search plane, hunting for people. He thought that so far it hadn't detected them.

He told Vita, "I don't think they spotted us in the water. I remember hearing Mom and Dad talk about it. They discussed whether or not the cooling effect of a wet body would counteract the scanning machine's search for warm spots. My dad said that unless a whale surfaced, the machine would not be able to spot it."

Vita said, "Then I guess we were okay."

"Yes, but what about No Name? Where do you think he

was when the plane circled? Do you think he hid? Or would he be taken in by their offer of food?"

Vita shrugged. "Who knows?"

Philip couldn't stop worrying. "Would No Name tell them we are here?"

She looked worried, too, as she sat up in her side of the sheltering bushes. "Really, Philip, I don't know."

"And his fire," Philip persisted. "Sometimes he builds a fire. The sensors would be sure to detect that."

She nodded. "Yes, I understand." Then she spoke of the moon again. "Tonight we will get the grunion and maybe No Name will be there, too."

Philip didn't question her about the fish; the plane was looping back over the top of the bluff. It wasn't until the drone of its second, more distant circle faded that they dared creep out and climb on up their trail.

By the time they reached the top the sun was setting; its rays reflected off the section of the aerotrailer's silvery roof left uncovered by the rockslide.

Hungry as they were, they ran, too late, Philip feared, to litter the roof with rocks so that the trailer would blend into the rockslide. Philip carefully shielded the space occupied by the seawater converter with a brown endurocloth blanket brought up from inside the aerotrailer, and, as they worked, explained to Vita about the converter.

"You see it isn't very big. Without its tank, it's portable. If you will help me lift it in a blanket, we can carry it with us if the time comes when we have to hide from the Scorpions."

Vita spread another shovel full of gravel as she answered. "Of course I will help you. It is my life, too. I understand the danger."

Philip hoped she did and now and then glanced up at the

mountain toward the bushes that marked No Name's camp. "Where do you think No Name could be? We've got to find him before he builds a fire."

"I know. I know." Vita said. "But he hunts. He fishes. He is still a wild boy. I do not know how to find him."

Philip nodded and stopped to look at the gravel-covered roof. "I think that's the best we can do. And do you know something?" He grinned.

Vita added a few stones to weigh down the blanket. "Know what?"

"I've been thinking of what the announcer on the plane said. He said they would be back tomorrow. And that means . . ."

Vita stood up and interrupted. "That means we can build a fire!" Her voice rose with excitement. "We will cook everything we can tonight to last us as long as we can make it last. Oh, Philip, hurry up and build a fire!"

In spite of their danger, Philip's interest turned to food. For the present, nothing else mattered. He thought he had never been this hungry.

After he had made the fire, he watched Vita put a kettle on to boil. When the hot rocks that surrounded the fire heated, she laid the black-shelled mussels there to steam open and reveal their succulent golden meat.

Following Vita's example, Philip folded mussels in his freshly baked corn cake and, when that was eaten, picked morsels from other shells, and sucked the contents of the sea urchins. The fragrance of the crabs, which had magically turned from brown to red in the boiling water, assailed his nose before Vita dipped them out. She showed him how to crack their shells on a stone and together they shared the delicious lumps of white meat.

They feasted.

For the second time since insta-meals failed him, Philip had enough to eat. And there was still more food. They stored what was left in plastic containers and prepared more by burying a pot of beans in the coals. Now in the days just ahead there would be no need to light a fire.

By the time they'd hidden the food from No Name, a white moon had risen high in the star-strewn, blue-black sky. It was then that Vita explained her further plans for that night.

She pointed to the stacked wood. "Philip, we will cook again on the beach tonight, so bring dry wood and matches."

His watch announced that it was past twelve when, armed with a flashlight and dressed in his warm soccer jacket and high socks, he shouldered his bundle of firewood and followed Vita, who disdained a light. Her back looked bulky in her thick black-and-white sweater.

At first he used his light and walked cautiously, listening to the pounding surf below. But when they reached the trail, Philip's eyes had adjusted to the night, and a flashlight was unnecessary. The moon cast enough light to allow them to pick out the path.

Halfway down, at Oscar's bushes, Vita paused. She cut each of them two green switches and told Philip, "These are for the grunion."

Philip said, "Thanks," but he didn't know what she meant. To him the night was becoming more and more unreal, but he continued his descent as if drawn by the rhythmic sound of the surf.

At the foot of the trail a glistening strip of mirrored moonlight continued the path far out to sea. They settled on the beach, just above the reach of the waves, and soon their fire joined the moon's reflection to brighten a shimmering stretch of wet sand.

Philip's ears had grown accustomed to the recurrent boom and running out of the surf, and in a silence between the crashing of the waves, he asked, "Why are we here?"

She studied the water's edge. Foam, as if lighted from within, glowed in layered curves against black water. "Wait. You will see. The fish will come."

"Why?" This didn't make sense. They had no hooks, just plastic bags and the switches cut from Oscar's bushes.

But he peered into the waves and saw glimmers brighter than the breakers rolling in on a wave. Three small, silver-blue, wriggling fish lay glittering on the sand.

Vita whispered a cheer. "Yay!" But she lifted her hand and sat down to watch. "The first ones are scouts. They come to look."

She slipped out of her sandals and socks and rolled up her pants, so Philip took off his shoes and socks, too.

Now flipping fish lay scattered all over the sand, and Vita leaped up. "It is time!"

She pounced, stuffing a fish into her bag, and Philip followed her.

A fish next to his foot squirmed, sinking its tail into the dark sand. Several fish encircled its head.

Vita explained. "It is laying eggs. At the next high tide, the eggs will hatch—become fish."

For a moment Philip watched, amazed. It didn't seem fair to pick up fish so smart they knew when to lay eggs for the next high tide. But he heard Vita shout at him.

"Pick them up! There are lots of them."

As a wave swept some fish out and deposited others, he

scooped one up. Its cold, slippery body squirmed in his hand. He felt a little sick, but he told himself, it is a fish, people eat fish, and pushed it into his plastic bag.

He picked up another, then drifted into the surf gathering them. He watched those on the sand flip out to meet each wave. He hated himself for what he was doing, but he knew he had to do it. Fish were food, and they had to try to get food wherever they could.

When they had bagged enough of the grunion, Vita stirred up the fire and showed Philip how to string them on the green switches for roasting.

When they had eaten their fill for the second time that night and packed the rest of the fish in plastic bags, they put on their shoes and socks. Philip's watch said two thirty, and he was groggy from too much food and too little sleep. Yet just as he was scooping up wet sand to put out the fire, worry crowded into his mind.

He threw an extra handful of wet sand on the dead bonfire, and called to Vita who was packing the bags of fish for them to carry. "Where is No Name? You said he would be on the beach tonight. Remember?"

In the dim moonlight, he saw Vita shrug. She said, "To-morrow I will find him. Tomorrow I will tell him."

"But . . ." Philip stared at her. Didn't she know tomorrow might be too late? Maybe she didn't fully understand how important it was to keep hidden. He thought he'd made it clear about the scanner. He tried again. But his voice seemed weak against the booming sea, and Vita hurriedly led the way up the bluff. Feeling helpless, he tagged along. He could only hope that No Name wouldn't signal their presence.

16 The View from the Mountaintop

It was a quarter to three in the morning when Philip and Vita, burdened by their bags of cooked grunion, climbed over the rocks that hid the entrance to the aerotrailer. Forgetting he had a flashlight, Philip stumbled sleepily about in the dark as they entered the kitchen for a before-bed drink. When he turned on the faucet, water splashed off something in the sink. What was it? He put down his glass and reached for the light. The sink was full of grunion.

Philip groaned. "Not more!"

But Vita was pleased. "No Name brought them. He did what I asked him to do. He brought us fish."

Big deal, Philip thought. The beach was covered with them. Then Philip listened for Vita's comments as she felt in the cupboards to check out the food they had stored. What had No Name helped himself to this time?

"It is okay," she said after a while. She turned to the door to glance toward the fire pit. "Maybe No Name ate some of the beans. Tomorrow we shall see."

Philip agreed. It was too late to dig up the buried pot of beans. But he didn't trust No Name. Before going to bed he studied the mountainside to make sure there was no fire to inform an early-morning plane of their presence.

Then he remembered the direction in which the plane had flown. It might have circled the smaller island he and Vita had seen from the mountaintop. Did someone live on that island? Perhaps people desperate enough to show themselves to that plane? Tomorrow he'd try to get Vita to climb the mountain with him.

But the next morning when Philip awoke it was already ten fifteen. And when he'd dressed in his shorts, socks, and shoes, he found that Vita wasn't there.

Calling her name, he ran outside. She was in the little meadow near the edge of the bluff. Her bent back was turned toward him, and she seemed to be digging.

After filling up on cooked grunion, some of them rolled in his alloted corn cake, and drinking his fill of cool water, he ran to see why she was digging.

When he reached the meadow, he saw that she had dug a small trench. In it she was planting both grunion and dry red beans. Philip stared at her in amazement. Of course he knew that beans grew from seeds. But fish?

Vita smiled at him. "The fish make the beans grow fast. No Name brought so many I had to use them." She glanced into the sky. "If we hide from the plane, we will need beans to eat."

Philip smiled back at her. "That is a smart idea." But how well hidden are we? he wondered. He asked Vita, "Have you seen No Name this morning?" He studied her closely because he knew that she would shield No Name.

She dug diligently and seemed not to hear.

"Come on, Vita," Philip said. "Tell me. Did No Name let the plane see him? Or did he hide?"

Vita shrugged. "He did not hide. But he said they did not see him. He says maybe they are friends. They speak the language of the Open Country."

"So what? That doesn't make them friends, does it? You

know about the Scorpions. You made sure No Name understands about them, didn't you?"

Vita nodded and shrugged again.

Philip was angry. But what could he do? The plane was coming back today. "I'll help you dig," he told Vita. He took the shovel out of her hands and dug furiously. He didn't tell her that he wanted to look for help on the other island.

The grass roots and soil were heavy, and the sun was warm. By the time Philip had dug a row half as long as Vita's, perspiration ran down his forehead. It trickled through his eyebrows and lashes and stung his eyes. His throat was dry, and the muscles in his arms and back hurt. But he knew Vita well enough to know that she wouldn't climb the mountain until her planting was finished.

She brought him water to drink and used a jug from the converter to soak the row of beans she had planted. Then she took back the shovel and sent him to carry out the other containers of water from their emergency store while she finished digging the row. "Like people," Vita said, "beans don't thrive on salt water."

When they hauled the empties back to the trailer, Philip realized that tomorrow they would be busy most of the day refilling them.

He was tired, and it was already past three o'clock in the afternoon when they finished. Nevertheless he felt he just had to ask Vita to climb the mountain with him to see if anyone lived on the other island.

To his surprise, she seemed delighted.

"Yes! What a good idea! Maybe they are friends. We will take matches to build a signal fire. If they have flour, we will trade. We will trade our water."

Philip had to smile at her cheery tone.

But as they started to climb the mountain, he no longer felt like smiling. His muscles ached from digging, and his mind ached with the memory of that terrifying night when he had last climbed this mountain. Every detail played itself back. How could he look south, where the blast of Central Power had turned the sky to flame, and still believe his parents or his home in the Towers survived?

When they reached the top of the mountain, the ravaged croplands he glimpsed in the distance appeared barren. Black rifts, only occasionally streaked with green, stretched beyond the horizon toward the Towers.

Tears came to Philip's eyes.

Before they fell he heard Vita's cheerful voice. "See!" She pointed to the island below them.

A telltale wisp of smoke rose from it.

Philip inspected the source of the smoke. It came from a small sheltered beach on the craggy island set in the swirling brown seaweed Vita called kelp. A few bushes smaller than those where No Name made his camp, and the same dry grass, dark-green plants, and cactus grew in patches between the stones.

He wondered who had built the fire. How could he tell if they were friend or foe? How could they help him keep No Name from signaling the plane? They were even more exposed.

Philip strained to see movement. Maybe a person. But the island was too far away.

Somehow it felt good to look down on a smaller island. But how did the person or persons on that small island feel about looking up at them? Of course they would want to come over.

Could a good swimmer reach them? No, Philip decided, they would need a boat.

He turned to Vita and saw that her expression had changed.

"There is no flour there," she said, shaking her head. She pointed to the kelp. "Maybe fish live in there, but none of the grains to make flour can grow in the rocks."

Philip agreed. There were no fields of corn or anything else. He saw with relief that Vita had no intention of building a signal fire.

He realized now that, without a regular food supply, friend or foe threatened their survival. Each day he and Vita struggled to keep themselves alive. He felt good about how well they had done so far. And he had done his part by making the seawater converter work.

On the way down the mountain Philip became aware of fog rolling in. From the ocean great pearly-white clouds curled toward them. There was something ominous about them.

Then a jolting thought crossed hs mind. He turned to Vita in panic.

"It is okay," she said. "Fog is nothing to worry about."

"But it is!" Philip cried. "We didn't refill the desalter!"

Now he remembered! During a whole month the area around the Towers had been fogbound. The sun had not come out once, and the stored supply of reclaimed water the people depended on ran out. Water had to be shipped in from the eastern Tower communities in aerotankers.

Philip gulped. Who would ship water in to him and Vita and No Name?

17

The Soccer-Jacket Bribe

Philip told Vita the details of how the solar desalter worked —about Jonesite and the water and the sun. But he realized that it must sound as strange to her as her story about the grunion had sounded to him.

Why hadn't he explained it to her before? She was smart about a lot of things. She would have understood. Then they wouldn't have used up most of their water supply on the beans. Now if they ran out of water, he had no one to blame but himself.

With Vita leading the way, they climbed down the mountain through the thick whiteness that drifted between them. It seemed to be trying to separate them, to enclose each of them in its watery walls.

When Vita reached a hand back to take his, Philip felt reassured. As long as he had Vita everything would turn out all right.

He tried to believe that tomorrow the fog would be gone—that the desalter would work again.

Back in the kitchen of the aerotrailer Vita refused to chance it. She carefully measured the purified water drained from the tank into three parts, filling three four-liter containers. "One is for No Name. He knows about some other wet things. Maybe he will bring them to us in trade."

Philip stared at her. What could they use more than water? And No Name—that dimwit! Sure, he knew how to hunt and fish, but he might already have endangered them all. And Vita didn't even seem to care. Anything that No Name did was all right with her.

No Name was foolish enough to think that the plane people were friends just because they spoke his language. Yet it was obvious they were the vigilantes who had murdered starving people. Why couldn't Vita persuade him?

Well, Philip thought, if Vita can't stop No Name, I'll have to think of a way to keep him from giving us away. Then he almost laughed aloud. No way could No Name signal that plane or any other plane through the dense whiteness that enclosed them now.

Another thought raised his spirits. Search planes had to regard the fog as an insurmountable obstacle to locating people.

The fog was a friend. If only they had been prepared!

Philip told Vita about it. He pointed overhead. "We can build a fire if we want. They can't see us."

Vita looked up from her dinner preparation. "Now why did I not think of that?" She laughed. "Philip, you can make a fire so we do not eat in the dark."

And for more than a month when the sun sometimes brightened the overcast at noonday but failed to lift it, they built fires to steam open mussels and clams. They gathered their own mussels from the fogbound rocks, and No Name delivered clams—the wet things—in the night. Flesh of these shellfish, along with the green sea spinach and the licorice-flavored fennel they often chewed because it killed their hunger, added welcome moisture to their diet.

Fog condensed on the aerotrailer roof trickled off uselessly until Philip contrived a way to gather some of it in plastic bags. The total yield was no more than a fraction of a liter, but he felt this accomplishment somehow redeemed his failure to refill the containers.

He rationed his water as, every day, with fading hope, he checked out Central Power. At the same time he tried to shut out the heavy weight that came into his middle whenever he thought of his parents. If they were alive, why didn't they come?

Then one day just past one o'clock in the afternoon, the sun penetrated the fog. Suddenly they were back to normal. By the tank the jugs full of seawater waited for the moment when the needed solar rays returned to bring out the magnetizing properties of Jonesite.

Vita's and Philip's eyes met. They stopped husking grain from the wild grasses they had gathered. Hastily they climbed up onto the trailer roof, turned the dials, and poured seawater into the tank. Soon the pleasant little grinding sound began that signaled salt was being magnetized out of the water.

"Yay!" Philip yelled.

"Hurray!" Vita cheered.

By four o'clock, when the fog closed in on them again, they had a full tank plus an extra four-liter jug for each of the three of them.

Vita picked up her jug. "I will water the beans," she said.

Philip followed with his jug. He'd drunk his fill; they had water to last them a week; and with only their present ration of half a corn cake, nothing seemed so delectable to Philip as Vita's beans.

Together, they admired the rows that had come up. At first, a few leaves had folded out to cup up toward the sun; now there were blossoms. But Vita appeared worried as she bent down to pour their treasured water into the trench next to the plants. She glanced at the sky. "It is the sun that makes them mature."

As Philip looked around, a wisp of breeze stroked his cheek. "Did the wind push the fog out to sea?" he asked Vita.

She stood up and pointed at the crouching gray wall above the ocean. "The wind does a dance. We cannot tell if it will twist and twirl the fog this way or that." She smiled at him. "I think this wind wants to dance at sea. Tomorrow the sun will shine."

Philip sighed. Vita was so wonderful. She knew so much.

Then he remembered. Tomorrow, if the sun was back, the fog would no longer hide them. They would have water. But, they would be exposed again. He felt like covering his head and running to hide with Oscar. Now the plane could find them, and they hadn't even persuaded No Name not to build fires. He questioned Vita about it over their dinner of cold cooked crab, raw spinach, and fennel.

Suddenly the unwashed figure of No Name appeared before them with two big fish. About half a meter long, their round silver sides gleamed in his dirty hands.

Vita beamed. "They are corbina," she told Philip.

He repeated, "Corbina?" and studied the fish.

He eyed No Name's stained hands. What would his mother think if he ate food touched by hands that dirty? Of course Philip knew he'd been eating clams and other shellfish No Name had traded for water, but they'd been left at night when Philip was asleep. He hadn't seen the hands that brought them.

In spite of the fish that meant a full stomach, Philip eyed No Name with distaste. His hair hung in jagged strands, as if he'd grabbed what interfered with seeing and hacked if off with his knife.

Philip ran his fingers through his own hair; Vita had helped him cut off some of his red-brown mop. And she had reminded him, as on that first day in the surf, to keep clean. And he wanted to. Keeping clean helped him believe his parents would return for him.

Vita laid the fish on the counter and admired them in Open Country language, gesturing about the length, the weight, the superior flavor of that kind of fish. Soon her knife flashed as she gutted and scaled.

"Tonight we will cook them," she told Philip, then turned to No Name asking for his approval.

"No!" No Name said. "I take mine. I cook."

Vita shook her head at him and spoke rapidly in No Name's language, then explained to Philip. "I told him the plane will see the fire. I will cook late when the plane has gone to sleep."

When No Name understood, he shook his head and snatched up his fish.

Vita turned to Philip and shrugged. "What more can I do?"

Philip glared at her and No Name. He thought, just when we are doing so well all on our own. But what could he do? How could he bribe No Name?

Then he remembered what Vita had said about No Name when he'd tied his clothes in knots. "It may be because he has never had clothes like yours."

Philip ran to get his soccer jacket and handed it to Vita. "Tell No Name he can wear it this evening. It is in trade for no fire." He disliked having his clean jacket worn by grubby

No Name, but he couldn't think of any other means of persuading him.

Vita glanced at No Name and stood tall. "No!" she told Philip. "No Name does not want the jacket."

No Name's eyes blazed. He dropped his fish and tried to snatch the jacket from Vita's hand.

Vita didn't let go as she spoke to Philip. "No Name is the wild boy. He does not care for Philip's clothes. He will not wash, keep clean, cut his hair." She turned No Name by the shoulder, and pushed him to see his reflection in the metal door of the useless refrigerator.

"See!" She pointed. "See the wild boy?"

No Name's shoulders drooped when he saw himself. "I go wash."

He laid the fish on the counter, turned, and raced toward the beach.

When he returned, hair slick, skin gleaming, he glanced angrily at Philip, grabbed the jacket, and ran up the mountain.

That very evening the plane came back, circling noisily overhead. This time the message was different. The harsh voice announced: "Liberation is at hand! Join with us and save yourselves. Food drop tomorrow." Again the words were repeated in Open Country language.

Cowering in the aerotrailer, Vita and Philip peered up at the plane from separate windows. The evening light touched its silver side, displaying the gammadion.

When danger of the scanner spotting them as a hot spot had passed, Philip joined Vita in the kitchen. He asked her, "What does he mean 'liberation'?"

She shook her head. "I don't know. But he said, 'join and

save yourselves.' Maybe we should do that. What chance do we have against them?"

Philip thought about it. Just two boys and a girl, it would be easy to hunt them down. Yet why should they do that? What was happening in the outside world? To him, one thing was clear: If these were the Scorpions, they had to be bad.

He spoke firmly. "As long as they don't know we are here, we are safe. I am sure of it." He turned on his watch and let Vita listen to the time with him. It was seven thirty-five. They decided to wait two hours before they cooked the fish.

At almost the same moment as the first flame blazed up, No Name, zipped to the chin in Philip's jacket, crashed down the mountainside. He sat beside the fire pit, arms folded, his square face held high, eyeing Vita's movements as she roasted his fish. Once it was ready, he ate swiftly and dropped the rest into the plastic bag he pulled from his pants pocket.

Vita watched him closely, and when he seemed ready to go, reminded him to leave the jacket.

As if Philip didn't exist, No Name peeled it off and laid it in Vita's hands.

Her body tensed as her eyes looked into his. The quick flood of her Open Country language told Philip that she was again warning No Name about the plane.

But to no avail.

No Name drew the gammadion in the air with his finger. "It is the friend," he said to Vita.

She told Philip. "He says it is the club of the wild boys." She shook her head. "That may be true, but there is more— much more. If I could only remember . . ."

She turned again to No Name, praising him for his goodness in bringing the fish to them. Then she pleaded with him until at last he nodded. As he left them and disappeared into the darkness, Vita said, "*Zogsi*," over and over.

Philip knew that meant "thank you," and added his *zogsi*. But still he wondered if Vita had persuaded No Name. Even with his comfortably full stomach, Philip worried about their safety as he fell asleep that night.

The next morning Philip's watch said ten seventeen when he and Vita started for the beach. The sun warmed them. They'd brought bags to gather mussels. But suddenly, halfway down, Vita froze on the trail.

Eyes wide, she pointed at the sea. Her voice, low and frightened, reached Philip above the roar of the pounding surf. "It is the red tide."

Philip recoiled at what he saw.

The beautiful sea had changed entirely. No longer did the breakers foam white out of clear greens and blues. Instead, the roiling waves surged out of turbid water turned to a muddy brown.

"What has happened?" he asked. The sea looked ugly, but not dangerous. Why did Vita seem so frightened?

She drew back and repeated. "The red tide has come!"

"So what?" Philip made an attempt to take charge. "Come on. We can still go down to the rocks and gather mussels."

Vita grabbed his arm. "No, no!" Her eyes blazed a warning at him. "We cannot eat the mussels. The red tide has made them poison!"

Philip tried to loosen her grip on his arm and back away. He gulped and stared. Only yesterday morning he'd eaten a mussel rolled in a corn cake for breakfast.

She hung on to his arm, digging her nails into it. "Deadly poison!"

Frantically, she looked up and down the beach. "No Name!" She called, half sobbing, "No Name! Brother!" She turned to Philip. "He has never seen the red tide. He will kill himself! He does not know!"

Over and over she called "No Name" and sometimes she called "Brother!"

18 Poison

Philip watched Vita's eyes as she searched the beach for No Name. She had wonderful, expressive eyes. She really cared about No Name. And what had she said? Was No Name really her brother? But how could that be? Vita was his relative. She spoke English. No Name was a wild boy. And that made Philip wonder. He asked, "Vita, why doesn't No Name know about the red tide? He knew about the grunion —about all the other wild things."

She shook her head. "He has never been to school. All he knows about is the Open Country. It is up here farther north that the red tide makes the mussels poison. Not the other shellfish—just the filter feeders—the mussels." She turned, her eyes clouded. "It may already be too late. But come on."

They raced up the bluff past the bean garden and picked their way through the cactus to No Name's camp.

Beside the mussel shells, now heaped high, and his sweater and blanket lay treasures No Name must have found on the beach. But No Name wasn't there.

Philip examined the collection curiously; he picked up a large iridescent shell with a row of six small holes in its side.

"That is an abalone shell," Vita said. "Abalone is very good to eat."

Scattered on a coil of yellow rope lay brown and green bottles topped by one shoe. Philip inspected the shoe. It looked like his own—striped with blue to match his soccer clothes—the one he'd lost in the surf with his parents. It was discolored and battered by the sea now. Of course, No Name never wore shoes.

Philip suddenly felt uncomfortable. He was a snooper. This was No Name's camp—these were No Name's things. He turned away wondering how it would feel to be No Name, to be a wild boy who had never even owned a pair of shoes.

He joined Vita at the edge of No Name's camp where she scanned the mountainside. She glanced at him and shook her head. Then, braid swinging, she began to lead the way down to the aerotrailer. Her voice sounded defeated. "If No Name is sick, he will come."

That evening, sitting by their fire pit, they silently ate their cold dinner. If Vita said the mussels had suddenly turned to poison, Philip believed her. He looked into her troubled face and asked about No Name. "Is he really your brother?"

Vita nodded. "I should have told you before. I would have told my cousin—your father. Or maybe your mother."

"Why not me?"

Vita studied him. "I thought you would not want him, would not understand. He is not like you. You see, in the

Open Country the government says there can be only one child. I am that child. I live at home, go to school. So when No Name came we had to hide him. He grew up wild."

"But, Vita," Philip said. "In my country, too, one child is advised. Only a few of my friends have a brother or a sister. But it is no crime."

Vita sighed. "I was afraid you would not understand."

"But I want to," Philip told her. "My parents said you'd be a sister to me. I think you are better than any sister I've ever heard about. You are good and kind—not only to me, but to No Name. I'm sure your parents were great people, too. So even though No Name couldn't live at home, why didn't they at least give him a name?"

Vita gave him her you-aren't-too-bright look. "Can't you see? It was for his own protection. If he was picked up by the authorities and questioned—even when he was a tiny child —he and all the other little children shook their heads and said "No name." In that way, by banding together, both the family and the child were protected. Do you understand?"

Philip grinned at her. "That was a smart idea—a very smart idea."

Vita smiled back. "And, of course, all the No Names could find their own families whenever they felt safe." Her smile faded and she looked down. "It was strange—very strange. I always felt guilty to be the one who got everything. That is, I got everything—school and a good home—up until the time of the drought and famine. Then my parents died."

Philip saw that Vita's eyes glistened with tears. He thought of the dreadful times Vita must have endured. How could she be so sweet and gentle when she'd gone through so much?

Then he thought of his own parents. Where were they?

He told Vita about his fears. "My mother and father may be dead, too." Voicing the awful thought made him choke up. "I d-don't know. Maybe they landed somewhere. Maybe they are safe. I hope so." Philip shook his head. "But even though they weren't close enough to be killed in the explosion when Central Power blew up, how would they live? The Tower people aren't like you. My mother wouldn't have the least idea of how to make a corn cake. And, of course they'd eat the poison mussels in the red tide. They wouldn't know." For a moment Philip bowed his head and held it in his hands as he tried to think. "I'm sure they wouldn't have known about the grunion."

Vita nodded. "I understand what you are saying and I hope they are safe. They seemed very kind. I talked to your mother on the telephone, and your father sent money to bring us up here."

"*You*," Philip corrected. "Bring *you* up here."

Vita nodded. "I know he knew of no one but me, but he worded the message: 'offspring of my cousin Henry' and that was how I was able to bring my brother. My country did not want him, and your country could not refuse him. But I did not know how your parents would feel about having another person to feed."

Philip nodded. He looked at the dead fire pit. They sat in the dark with only the stars and a sliver of moon for light, but he felt that he and Vita were seeing one another better than ever before. He told Vita, "Now I understand why you didn't meet them at the border—why you came on the aerobus." Philip looked lovingly at Vita. "Thank goodness you came. Without you I'd be dead." He tried to laugh. It wasn't funny.

But Vita did laugh. Then abruptly she stopped. "If I had gone to the border, I would be dead too."

"We are both lucky," Philip said.

In answer, she reached for his hand, and he moved to put his arm around her.

She smiled at him and said, "I cannot think of anyone I would rather be with in an earthquake."

He squeezed her arm, and they went on to discuss that dreadful night, and as they talked a raccoon searched for crumbs. Sometimes they'd fed mussels to the raccoon, opossum and skunk. Did the little animals know they could be poison?

Philip asked Vita, but she shrugged absentmindedly. Again she became restless. She jumped up. "I have got to find No Name. Let us look on the beach."

So, dressed as they had been for the grunion hunt, they started down the dark trail.

At the spot where they could see the shoreline spread below them, Vita stopped.

Philip peered around her and gasped. The bands of surf rolling in seemed filled with millions of Fourth-of-July sparklers. He stood spellbound, heart thumping, as he gazed at the astonishing scene. "Vita! Look! What is it?"

Vita said. "At night the red tide is very pretty."

" 'Pretty!' It's more than pretty. It's fantastic! Okay to go look?"

"Sure," she said and raced ahead of him down the trail.

On the beach, they shed their shoes, and just before they reached the water's edge, Vita stopped and pointed to her foot. "Look!" she said as she placed it on the wet sand and stepped onto what instantly became a disk of white light that glowed like a fallen moon. Then she ran leaving a path of fading moons behind her.

Philip shouted with joy as light sprang up around his

footprints in the wet sand. It was crazy, spooky, fantastic! He ran, a path of lightning following his wake. He dragged his toes and scattered sparks. Then a wave caught him, and the sea flashed. Wildly he swept his hands in arcs to ignite the water and called, "Look, Vita! I'm electric! A whole power station!"

Then unexpectedly, the Scorpion plane, lights blinking, zoomed down from out of the darkness over their heads. Quickly they hid in the chilly waves. But Philip saw that the water flashed white around both him and Vita. He shivered with fear as he realized what that meant. Their presence was revealed as plainly as if a spotlight were turned on them.

But the plane banked and turned.

As soon as the drone faded, he and Vita, clothes dripping, grabbed their shoes and raced for the bushes. Halfway there they heard the plane returning, prepared for another sweep.

Breathless, they reached the bushes and hid. Then Philip parted the branches to look down at the beach and saw a figure racing along the edge of the surf. It was No Name! And he was dragging his feet in the wet sand, leaving blazing white marks—signals easily read from above!

19 Hiding

Philip raged as, from their hiding place in the bushes, he and Vita watched the plane, signal lights blinking, settle onto the beach. Its engines continued to hum, shutting out all other sounds. A door slid open, silhouetting No Name's sturdy form in a patch of light. Then, from inside the plane, a heavy arm reached out toward him, clutching, as if meaning to pull him aboard.

No Name dodged into the darkness. But, like the hungry raccoons they fed, he returned. He stood motionless, ready to flee, nodded, seemed to listen, then gestured toward the bluff.

Again the hand reached. This time No Name ran—racing toward their path.

Instantly the plane became airborne, lights flashing. It buzzed angrily away into the night sky.

On the trail below, Philip heard gravel slide under No Name's feet.

Vita was waiting for him, crouched like a cat ready to spring.

But Philip pounced first. As if No Name were a soccer ball, he butted him in the stomach, yelling, "You dirty, rotten guy!"

No Name shrieked, gasped, and fell backward, rolling down the trail. Philip dragged him up, pounding on him until Vita pulled him off.

Her firm hand clutched the back of his shirt. "Philip, you are not the wild boy. You must not do this." Then she freed him and hauled No Name to his feet. She spat words into his face both in Open Country language and in English. After she'd told him what a traitor he was, and how he had endangered all of their lives, she asked, "Did you tell him we are here?"

Speaking English, No Name seemed to make an effort to equal the impact of her words. "He is the friend. He bring us guns! We need it, he bring us a boat." Clutched in Vita's threatening grip, he screamed, "He bring us flour! We need the flour!"

Vita let him go, and he scrambled on up the path.

She called after him, "We shall see if the friend brings the flour." It wasn't until just before he disappeared into the darkness that Vita warned him about the red tide and poison mussels.

Then, their climb slowed by worry, Philip and Vita plodded up the trail. It was then that Vita turned to Philip, her face sad. "Too late I remember. The gammadion. Now I know what it is."

"Yeah?"

"Did you ever hear of the murderer, Falkin? He was a very bad man. It was his emblem. The Scorpions started with Falkin." She groaned. "Now what do we do? If the Scorpions come here and take our food and water, we will die."

Philip tried to cheer her. "They may not come right away." He clung to the belief that his parents would return and save them. As he had so often before, he looked up at the sky, hoping to see the line of sky traffic that would mean the world was normal again.

Then he thought of practical matters and told Vita, "Now that they know someone is here, we don't need to worry about our fire. I counted the matches. Only eleven are left. You know how to bank the fire so that it will burn day and night. Right?" He waited for her nod and went on, "Driftwood is always washing up on the beach. There is no reason to let the fire in the pit go out, is there?"

Vita nodded, but Philip knew she wasn't persuaded that anything about their situation was good. Nor was he.

If the scout plane reported that their island was habitable, they might make a base of it. Certainly the mainland was ravaged. And, if they came, there was no way the supply of plants and animals could feed them. As it was, without mussels to eat, their own food supply would be curtailed. Philip groaned and looked at the sharp angle of Vita's jaw and ran his fingers over his bony ribs.

"Tell me about the mussels—how long will it be before we can eat them?"

Vita's steps became brisker, her voice more assured. "After the red tide goes, at least two weeks." As they neared the aerotrailer she explained about the other shellfish that were harder to find, such as the spiny lobster. "Tomorrow there is much to do to hide our house. But the next day we will fish."

From seven in the morning the following day they worked to conceal their whereabouts. By now the path to the beach was so well trodden that there was no way to disguise it, but once the rockslide surrounding the trailer was reached, only a practiced tracker could spot the way.

A suggestion of a trail led up the mountainside into the cactus surrounding No Name's camp. With the shovel, Philip and Vita took turns smoothing and improving this path in the hope that a false start into the evil barbs would discourage intruders. Since the fire pit and bean patch couldn't be disguised, they decided other decoy trails leading into the cactus might be useful to gain time.

As they labored anxiously, the seawater converter was working to provide water for the beans and to fill the containers and tank. Once, around two o'clock, they heard the hum of the Scorpions' plane, but it dropped no flour for No Name. In fact, the sound remained distant, and Vita and Philip, poised to hide, nodded an I-told-you-so at each other when the drone ebbed.

The next day, after a scanty breakfast of fishbone and spinach soup and half a corn cake each, they planned their diving expedition. Philip's mouth watered when he remembered the lobster No Name had brought them. Its flesh had been hearty and delicious. But Philip knew No Name dived deep to capture it. Every day he went to this special place— more often than not without luck.

Today, wearing swim trunks, Philip planned to dive, too. Vita pointed to the cove in the bluff that No Name had described. The day was warm, and the sea seemed to be telling them it was a lake.

But when they arrived, Philip's down-elevator feeling sucked him in as he searched the water's depths. The rock wall buckled inward shading the swirling green below from the sun's direct light; seaweed, grown into underwater trees, waved beckoning arms at him. A fish's bulging gold eyes gazed angrily at him before it slung its tail and wallowed away.

Philip didn't like it. And as he and Vita slipped in and swam in circles, he sensed something strange about her. Was it lack of confidence? No use asking. She would never admit it.

He watched fearfully as, after a few exploratory underwater swims, she surfaced and told him. "You wait. First I will try." She drew her knife.

He felt forsaken as he watched her flutter her legs, kick, and push her arms through the seaweed to find her way lower and lower, until she disappeared from sight in the ever darker depths.

Endless seconds passed. Where was Vita? How could he wait? He dived. Swimming underwater, he searched for her and was suddenly aware of a sleek body plummeting past him. His ears throbbed. His heart pounded. He felt his chest would burst before he surfaced.

After inhaling deeply, he dived again and, at last, saw Vita. Her hand trailed a spiny lobster. She wasn't alone. No Name was pushing her upward. Just before she surfaced the lobster fell away.

Gasping, Philip reached for her, slung one arm under her, and, carried by a wave, tumbled her onto the beach. The next wave delivered an anxious-looking No Name with the lobster.

No Name shrieked when saw Vita's open mouth, closed eyes, and colorless face. Instantly he tipped her chin up, pinched her nose and began breathing into her mouth.

When her chest, at last, moved for a time on its own, he briskly rubbed her hand.

Helpless and frantic, Philip stood over them. He was about to kneel and rub the other hand, when he glimpsed something beyond the breakers. Stifling a cry, he ducked his head.

A boat was moving toward them—a skiff rowed by six hollow-eyed near skeletons with wildly straggling hair. It was no more than fifty meters away.

Philip felt his fingers turn into claws as he clutched No Name's shoulder and pointed.

20 The End of Oscar

When No Name saw the skiff with its ghastly crew, his eyes mirrored Philip's panic.

They both flashed glances at the bluff, and Philip saw that No Name, too, was assessing their chances of hiding up there. He shook his head, and Philip agreed. There was no way to move Vita. The water was their best means of concealment.

Together, they dragged her into the surf. As her eyes turned slowly from one to the other and fell shut, they swam, flailing their legs, floating Vita on their hands, until they reached the deep shade of the bluff.

There, silently treading water and hidden by the rocks, they watched and listened.

Querulous voices identified the boat's occupants as both men and women. Before they splashed ashore, they reached into the skiff to arm themselves with rifles that bore the emblem of the Scorpions on their stocks. Once they had dragged the skiff onto the beach, they spotted the trail and rushed toward it without looking back.

Philip and No Name now dared to turn their attention to Vita. She moaned but the eyes in her pale face remained closed. No Name felt her hands and arms and shook his head. "She too cold."

Philip peered toward the plastic boat, empty except for two sets of oars turned inward on their locks. Suddenly he knew what to do. He could save Vita! But what if one of the group straggling up the trail turned? He forced himself to wait.

He heard the boat people shout to one another in English, and their conversation made plain to Philip the danger they were in.

Between the surges of waves, fragmented bits of conversation reached them. "... only a boy... take over... water... bigger than our island..." Next came an enumeration of the kinds of animals to be killed for food.

Then Philip and No Name were jolted by the crack of a rifle.

Excited voices yelled, "Rabbit!" followed by grunts of satisfaction and a shrieking argument.

Philip gulped at the realization that Oscar must have been blasted into bloody bits... bloody bits that these wild people were eating raw!

Philip saw No Name gulp, too, and felt that for the first time, eye to eye in the chill water, he and No Name understood each other.

When the skiff's occupants had disappeared above the bluff, No Name, as if directed by Philip's thoughts, floated Vita to where they could hoist her into the boat. Warmth from the hot sun beating on the plastic told Philip that here was her best chance to revive.

For a moment she responded to being dumped into the boat. Her eyes flew open. In unison, No Name and Philip told her, "Stay here!" Then they had to leave her.

As if of one mind, Philip and No Name streaked up the rockslide on the hidden side of the bluff. There was no purpose in trying to escape without the desalter.

Once they had come within earshot of the boat people,

they sneaked behind the aerotrailer. On hands and knees they crept among the rocks on the way to the roof.

Here, high enough to look down on the group, they peeked between rocks and saw them heedlessly trample the beans, and, in spite of the warm sunshine, huddle around the smoldering fire pit.

On the roof, Philip and No Name labored quietly, undoing the clamps that held the desalter in place. At the same time, they caught shreds of the invader's conversation. They were complaining. They had expected more. ". . . stupid kid said lots of water here . . . where is it?"

Their voices faded, as, following the path, they straggled up the hillside into the cactus.

Philip and No Name had nearly finished when they dared to peek to be sure they had all gone. They were disappointed to see that one woman remained. She wandered toward the beans, bent to lift a broken bush, picked and ate an unripe bean. She giggled to herself as she lifted plant after plant, stripping them, stuffing raw beans into her mouth. Then, furtively, she glanced around before filling the pocket of her ragged smock.

Philip raged at her for destroying Vita's precious beans, long before they were mature enough to harvest. But he stifled his anger at No Name for telling the Scorpions that water was plentiful. This was not the time for anger. Only by working together could they save themselves and Vita.

Creeping silently down the side of the aerotrailer, the two of them lowered the converter wrapped in its blanket. Now they were in plain view of the group on the mountainside. Why didn't the surf boom? No sound except the distant mild slosh of waves against the sand broke the silence. Philip thought, Surely we will be heard!

His body tensed, ready for action, but both he and No Name seemed to sense that the moment for their escape had not yet come.

They could see the bean woman sitting beside the fire, watching her companions scattered above her among the cactus. Her eyes seemed to be straying as if she had heard something.

Then a kind of cheer went up on the mountainside.

Philip and No Name didn't wait. The discovery of No Name's camp gave them the cover of noise they needed. Scampering, sliding down the rocks, they pushed the converter to where they could load it in the skiff.

Tossing the lobster aboard, they pushed off into the surf. Philip took the prow position while No Name swung the oars. Philip, who had never rowed anything but the dinghy in the Tower's pool, lifted his oars, awaiting No Name's instructions.

Vita, now roused, sat up. She seemed oblivious to Philip's orders to lie down. "Vita! Vita!" he whispered. "Duck!"

He felt relief flood over him, as, rowing mightily, No Name flashed them out to sea. Poised to row, Philip watched No Name's back in an effort to see how to handle the oars.

Then they were discovered. An outraged scream rose from above them. "They're stealing our boat!" Bullets sprayed, jetting the water around them.

Copying No Name, Philip frantically dipped the oars. The boat slowed. No Name shouted angrily, "I do it!"

Philip lifted his oars and the boat returned to life, skimming the water.

But there was one last shot. Vita's hand flashed to her forehead and fell away; her head lolled like a sleeping baby's.

Philip muffled a scream. Vita had been hit! But he didn't dare move from his palce.

No Name's strong arms powered the oars to move the skiff forward, but they seemed to get nowhere as blood trickled down Vita's cheek.

21 They Shot Vita!

Vita! Vita! Philip cried silently. Please don't die! Please!

Then he saw that No Name had rowed them out of danger so he gasped out the words: "They hit Vita! Her head's bleeding!" Behind him the oars faltered momentarily.

"You row," No Name said.

Philip dipped his oars and felt the boat come under his control as it moved first right then left as he strove to keep it pointed toward the island.

No Name had rested his oars, turned and crept up to examine Vita's forehead. When he had washed off the blood, Philip sighed with relief. The bullet hadn't penetrated: instead it had peeled off a narrow band of skin. He told No Name, "Not too bad."

But Vita remained ashen.

No Name shook his head. "Is bad!" Again he tested for body warmth and chafed her hands and feet. Then, hot though the sun was, he covered her with the brown blanket they had used to haul the desalter.

Philip nodded approval. Why hadn't he spotted the symptoms? The soccer team had learned all about it. Vita was in shock! Nearly drowning had been bad enough without being shot, too. He trembled as he looked at her. The only person in the world he had left that he cared about lay there dying. He loved her. What could he do without her?

They rowed through the kelp to reach the other island, and it was easy to see that the skiff full of skeletons had come from here. Mingled with the brown seaweed on the fine sandy beach was a litter of containers obviously left from the Scorpions' food drop. The fire still burned; the sand bore scars of the boat's launching. The remainder of the island was trampled—almost completely barren.

Even though it lay in the shadow of their own towering island—too close for comfort—they had no choice. Vita was hurt, perhaps even dying. To save her life they had to risk a stop.

Philip's watch said four fifty when they beached the skiff. It was getting late, and although the blanket would ward off the worst of the night's chill, a fire and hot food were essential to warm Vita.

The blaze of sun dropping toward the sea made Philip aware of his own lack of clothing. He rubbed his now tanned and freckled shoulders. He was wearing his endurocloth swim trunks, and Vita and No Name were in their shorts. All of them had stripped for diving. The fire would feel good.

Vita remained dazed as No Name and Philip gently led her ashore. Huddled in the blanket, she seemed grateful to sink into the warm sand beside the fire.

Philip felt comforted to see that the fire consisted of two large driftwood logs that only needed pushing together to ensure warmth throughout the night. Tomorrow, if Vita was able, they'd row south toward the Towers. How long it would take to get there, Philip didn't know. But he reasoned that, even though the Scorpions claimed to be liberators, the commandeering of their island indicated that some other government controlled the vast region to the south. There must be some people unfriendly to the Scorpions who would help them.

That late in the day the desalter worked more slowly but the sun still shone into the aperture long enough for them to catch drinks in their cupped hands. Yet how could they save some water for Vita? Philip wondered aloud.

No Name shrugged. "It is no problem. You find tin can on the beach. I find the shell."

They ate the lobster baked over the coals that night, awakening Vita long enough to make her swallow a few bites and take a few sips of water from the lobster shell.

During a restless night on the sand, Philip sometimes roused long enough to watch No Name offer Vita water and tuck the blanket around her.

The next morning, before Vita awakened, they ate steamed clams—large, tough clams that provided sweet meat to chew on and the promised shells to drink from.

"Where did you find them?" Philip asked.

No Name grinned and pointed to the beach a few meters from the fire. "Is lots of them."

Philip thought of the walking skeletons. Food had been right under their feet—if only they'd known. But he hadn't known it either. "Really? How can you tell? Will you show me how to find them?"

As he answered "yes", he eyed Philip's watch.

Philip held it to No Name's ear and watched the delight on

his face as he listened. Then he unbuckled it and handed it to him. "You can wear it for a while."

With a big grin No Name strapped the watch on his wrist and admired it—lifting it high, over and over punching the button that made the canned voice announce the time. Then he returned to the clams that had steamed open on the hot rocks next to the fire. Onto meat in the largest shells he laid seaweed. Then he unsheathed his knife and after sharpening it on a stone, swiftly minced the clam meat and seaweed so that juice sprang out of the clam—the juice that had so often saved them from the need for precious water. Next No Name replaced the top shell and carefully set the "stew" on the hot rocks to simmer.

Philip's watch on No Name's wrist drew his attention to the knife in his hand. What a wonderful thing a knife was! He remembered all of the things Vita did with hers and he asked No Name, "Sometime will you let me wear your knife—just for a few minutes?"

No Name's square face lighted with surprise. "You like my knife? I did not know." Quickly he unbuckled his belt and handed knife and belt to Philip.

Philip thought as he strapped the belt on, No Name is really a good guy.

For a moment he patted the hip with the knife in its sheath lying against it. Then he took it off and handed it back. "In my country we aren't allowed to wear knives." He grinned at No Name. "I just wondered how it felt. Thanks."

When Vita awakened, the skin around the dark wound on her forehead glistened yellowish-purple, and her eye had swollen shut. But she seemed glad to eat the fragrant clam stew No Name had prepared. Then, refusing help, she eased herself up onto her feet and walked a few steps in the heavy sand before she sat down again and asked, "What happened?"

Both Philip and No Name tried to tell her, and her un-swollen eye grew larger and larger as she listened. She sounded like herself again when, smiling, she looked from one to the other and said, "You two saved me! I love you both."

That wasn't really true about his saving her, Philip thought. No Name had saved them all. He had known just what to do when Vita came close to dying of shock. And without No Name's skillful handling of the skiff's oars, they would all have been shot. True, No Name had invited the trouble, but that was all in the past.

Now they had to look to the future. There was nowhere to go but south to the Towers. Philip hoped everything would be as he left it. But he knew that was wishful thinking. Remembering the flaming sky over Central Power and the empty fields they had seen from the top of their mountain, Philip worried about what they would find. Certainly no food for a while. He explained his fears to Vita and No Name, and asked, "If there is nothing left of the Towers, what shall we do?"

Vita answered, "There are islands and the Open Country. But first we must think of the food."

They all agreed. So, at the next low tide, Philip helped No Name dig several days' supply of clams and found a patch of miraculously untrampled sea spinach all on his own. Using the plastic containers left in the rubbish, as well as the clamshells, they packed the available food into the skiff and filled the additional jugs with fresh water.

Philip's watch on No Name's wrist announced that it was

two o'clock. They were just about to load the salt-water converter when they heard a frightening sound. It was the hum of a plane—unmistakably the Scorpions' plane. Now, where could they hide?

22 The Hot Spot

Philip screamed at No Name. "Help me!"

Why hadn't he thought of the plane? The boat! Laden with their supplies, it would betray them.

The plane was landing at the other island. It was only a matter of time before the skeletons told on them. Once the pilot learned that they had stolen the boat, the search would be on.

There was nothing to do but sink the boat—bury it beneath the waves. No Name showed Philip how. They rocked it madly, and laden as it was, it promptly disappeared from sight under the waving kelp.

On the beach, Philip saw that the brown blanket that covered the converter was indistinguishable from the brown seaweed draped here and there on the sand. But he remembered the electronic sensors on the scanner and yelled, "Hide by the fire! It's the hot spot!"

There, before the plane circled toward them from its landing on the other island, they topped their heads with seaweed, lay down, and buried themselves and Vita up to their chins in sand. Philip dug in on one side of the fire, No Name and Vita on the other.

Twice, zooming low, the plane's engines blasted their ears, its exhaust whirled nearby sand, and on Philip's side of the fire, fanned the coals into flame next to his head.

He screamed as the seaweed under which he had hidden steamed, dropping scalding drops down his face—searing streaks on his cheeks. Acrid smoke scorched his nostrils, stung his lungs. But he dared not move.

In a haze of pain, Philip saw that the plane was ready to set down. But, at the last moment, its landing wheels retracted and it veered off. None too soon. The plane roared away at the very moment Philip could bear the heat no longer.

He leapt from the ground, shed seaweed and sand, and tore into the surf to cool his tortured head. Vita, helped by No Name, followed. Unaware of Philip's burned face, they splashed themselves and each other.

Philip cupped his face in his hands in order to speak without hurting. "That was close!" He felt sure the pilot would have risked a landing, even in the heavy sand, if he'd had any suspicion they were there.

Vita and No Name laughed at their cleverness. But Philip knew they understood they were still in danger. Vita staggered to collapse and rest by the converter, and No Name and Philip dived underwater to try to pull the skiff out of the kelp bed. Little by little they edged it toward shore. At last, with No Name pushing and Philip pulling, they managed to beach it, bail out the water and rescue most of their clams.

It was dark when No Name and Philip again pushed the boat through the surf with Vita tucked safely aboard. Although Philip's muscles ached from yesterday's unaccustomed rowing and the scalded stripes on his face burned hideously, he was on his way to the Towers. He couldn't control his eagerness. To be heading home was a dream come true.

In a few hours his excitement was gone. His face had become a flaming torch, throbbing painfully. Rowing made his head reel—his strokes grew more and more unsteady. But they had to get out of the Scorpion plane's range and reach the Towers. He rowed doggedly.

At last his rowing became so erratic that No Name forced him to lie down in the bottom of the boat next to Vita. As the boat trundled gently in the waves, Philip felt No Name lay a cool pack of seaweed on his face, but he hurt too much to thank him. Dimly he thought he understood what No Name said in Open Country language as he tended first Vita, then him: "First is the sister—then the brother."

Was No Name calling him "brother"? Philip felt a kind of healing seep through him at the sound of the word. Since the moment they had first seen this skiff that No Name rowed so skillfully, the wall of anger that separated them had melted away; their thoughts had become as one. He remembered all the times since then, when, side by side, they'd worked to save themselves and Vita. As he mused on the bond that had grown between them, the pain of his burning face was submerged in soothing thoughts of his future life with Vita and No Name. His mind whirled into sleep.

At times during the following day, Philip awakened into a hazy, red daze to feel a cup pressed against his lips and hear No Name pleading with him to drink, or the comforting coolness of freshly dipped seaweed on his face. He wasn't sure how much time had passed when he again became aware of their position on the coastline.

He sat up in the bottom of the boat and at once saw that something was very wrong. The ever-dry coastal hills had turned from burned gold to scorched silver—even the ovals of the hardy *nopales* had tumbled into shredding gray heaps.

Vita, apparently her old self again, was rowing. Like No Name, she seemed to have rowed all her life, and the skiff vibrated gently over blue-green ripples as they flashed forward.

Philip checked out the rest of the boat. Beside the converter stood plastic containers filled with water. And buried under wet seaweed were lumps that Philip knew must be the big, hard-shelled clams they had dug on the little island. Food and water . . . for how long?

Then Philip saw that they were heading for a rocky cliff similar to the one where they had so often gathered mussels and crabs. Yet when they reached the rocks, there were no mussels—not even barnacles. No Name dived and speared a fish with his knife. But its flesh was flaccid, foul-smelling. Vita threw it back.

For dinner No Name's knife laid open two clams for each of them. Even raw, Philip found them delicious. However Vita closely inspected those that remained, turning them over doubtfully. "Tomorrow is the last day we can eat them." She shook her head. "Too many days have passed. They will be spoiled."

Now Philip took his turn rowing. How much farther was it? No Name and Vita began to speak uncertainly of the Open Country, and Philip sensed that beyond his goal was theirs.

They rowed through the night. By morning Philip began to wonder if they would reach either of their goals. At last, far in the distance, a pattern of sloping spires, like the black posts of a giant fallen fence, clustered against the sky. As they rowed on, forever and ever, it seemed, they came into the bay by the Towers. There Philip saw that what he had pictured on that dreadful night was indeed true. This was all that remained of the Towers, a grotesquely burned-out framework, the skeletal shell of his former home.

Numbed by disappointment and fright, they allowed the skiff to wash closer. Philip knew, but couldn't comprehend, this wasteland. He looked up at what might have been the 209th floor of Tower 117—his home—as No Name and Vita rested their oars. Then he heard Vita's voice spell out a word: "C-O-N-T-A-M-I-N-A-T-E-D." She read on, "DO NOT COME ASHORE!"

It was a sign—a huge sign. How had he missed it?

Philip couldn't control his tears. He sobbed and swore. Over and over he said the worst words he had ever heard. Why had this happened? How could it have happened? All his friends had lived here. Now they were all gone! And his parents! Where were they?

He felt somewhat comforted to hear No Name repeating what seemed to be the same swear words translated into Open Country language. Vita sobbed with him.

At last they realized that there was nothing for them in this spot. They swung on the oars, circling to return to the sea and turn their backs on the tragic scene. They looked south.

South was the Open Country—their only hope.

23 Return to the Towers

Philip couldn't stop crying as he took his turn at the oars. The soaring black spires on the ash-covered landscape told him what he had long known but had refused to believe. The Towers and everyone in them had been incinerated when Central Power blew up.

If he and his parents hadn't moved to the Wilderness Preserve, they would be dead, too.

And maybe his parents *were* dead, but he hated to abandon hope. Yet they'd been programmed for the border, less than twenty-five kilometers south of the Towers. How could they have escaped?

Philip shivered. The oars shook, and Vita, whose turn it was to rest in the bottom of the boat, gazed up at him and offered to take his place. "Come lie down, Philip. Close your eyes and forget it."

He refused her offer, but, as if a warm quilt had been wrapped around him, her effort to comfort him stopped his shivering. He rowed more steadily, trying to keep up with No Name, who seemed to be a machine as he stroked evenly on and on. At the same time he listened to what he knew was a staged conversation between Vita and No Name. Knowing that they were cheering themselves with their efforts to cheer him helped Philip to calm himself.

Vita spoke to No Name at some length in Open Country language.

No Name nodded his shaggy head, and Vita translated. "I asked him if he had ever heard of the Island of the Mussels, and if he knew where it was."

No Name talked over his shoulder. "Is nothing but mussels there."

"The island is encrusted with them," Vita said. "That is where we will go. It is said to be one of the coastal islands."

In spite of himself, Philip's mouth began to water. Even raw mussels seemed delectable. He pictured the masses of blue-black shells that could be opened to reveal succulent golden meat.

"We will row out of the bay and down the coast. It is not too far," Vita said.

Philip clung to the oars, trying to row more strongly and firmly toward their new goal. He felt the menace of the grotesque skeletal shapes of the Towers looming above him. After sighting them it had taken them almost half a day to reach them. It would take as long to leave them behind.

I won't look back—won't remember the Towers, Philip told himself. Trying to match his strokes to No Name's, he pushed forward, listening to the soft sound of lapping waves and the rhythmic creak of the oarlocks.

Suddenly these gentle sounds faded, absorbed in an encompassing surge of programmed music. The music engulfed Philip and his whole world.

"What's happening?" he yelled. Was he dreaming? He glanced hastily at Vita and No Name. It was clear that they heard it, too. Eyes wide, Vita sat up. No Name rested the oars and turned his head to gaze up at the Towers. "Who is it? Who makes the music?"

Vita's voice was frightened. "Is it the Scorpions?"

Yes, Philip thought, it could be the Scorpions trying to lure them ashore into the contaminated area. But no! That was silly. The Scorpions could have killed them all days ago if they had been hunting for them. "I don't know," he said. "I don't think it is the Scorpions. It sounds like the piped music in the Towers. But how could that be?"

No Name's head tilted as he listened to the music. A slow grin spread over his face, and his shoulders began to move to the tune. Then he picked up the oars and guided the skiff toward shore.

"No! No! No Name!" Vita crept back to grab his arm. "We cannot go ashore. It will kill us. And besides"—she pointed to the top of the Towers—"the music is coming from there. How do we get up there?"

Philip studied the blackened bones of the Towers. Could it be that the insulated part of the sound system had, by some miracle, saved it from incineration? "You're right!" he said to Vita. "The music is coming from up there. The broadcasting transmitter is working."

Suddenly he understood. "Vita! Do you know what that means?" In his excitement Philip half stood and nearly capsized the boat. "Central Power has come in!" He studied the sky. All afternoon little pompom clouds had been marching down from the north. Now they were closing ranks. But between them flashed a glitter high above.

Philip shrieked, "An aerocar! We're back to normal! We're saved!"

"Hurray!" Vita cheered.

No Name echoed her loudly. "Ray!"

Then, while the skiff, unattended, washed back and forth with the tidewater, they all sat with their heads tipped back, searching the sky for aerotraffic between the clouds.

114

Vita spoke loud enough to be heard above the programmed music. "They cannot see us."

Philip had to agree. "We can barely see them. The aerocars are too high."

So they weren't saved after all. Nothing had changed for them except the music. They were still three starving kids afloat in a skiff.

Who could help them? Philip thought of his parents. If by some miracle they had survived, they would hunt for him first at Shark Tooth Mountain. Then here. He explained to Vita, adding, ". . . and maybe the regular search planes will look for survivors by the Towers and try to save them from being contaminated."

Vita glanced soberly at the blackened shores and nodded.

At that moment No Name yelled, "Look!"

A large aerocar plummeted out of the sky. They identified it as an aeroambulance by the red cross on its bottom as it hurtled down.

At first it seemed aimed at them, but then it disappeared behind the land barrier to the south.

In a short time it rose to ascend. They waved frantically and yelled their lungs out.

But as the aeroambulance shot up into the clouds, all of Philip's high hope turned into despair.

In utter discouragement, all three of them slumped into their seats. Without speaking, Philip and No Name rowed just hard enough to keep them from running ashore.

Late in the afternoon the pale sun peeked out from the clouds long enough to set in the sea ahead of them. Philip touched his watch, and Vita and No Name leaned forward to hear it announce ". . . six fifty-eight and ten seconds."

"Too dark for them to see us," Vita said. "We will just have to keep on rowing until daylight."

Philip gulped. "You mean all night?" With the awful emptiness in his middle he didn't know if he could last all night. He drank from the plastic jug and felt the water slosh around in his stomach.

Vita settled herself under the brown blanket. "My turn rowing comes soon."

No Name guided the skiff to where, with the minimal movement of an oar, they could maintain a safe distance from shore.

Soon Philip found the persistent, soothing music lulling him to sleep. To keep awake and to revive his spirits he talked to No Name. "What are you going to do when we are rescued?"

"Eat," No Name said.

Philip laughed. "I know. Me, too. But after that?"

No Name shrugged. "First I take a name. I think about that a lot. Which you like: George or Henry?"

Philip thought about it. Henry was No Name's father's name. "I like both of them. But I guess you've got to decide that for yourself." In the dark he half saw, half pictured the slow ripple of the muscles in No Name's shoulders as he rowed. He told No Name, "When we are saved, maybe you could go to school with me and learn to play soccer. You'd make a great soccer player."

No Name nodded. In halting English, he described a soccer match he and the other wild boys in the Open Country had watched.

When No Name stopped talking, Philip was too exhausted to make the effort to continue the conversation.

On and on the music played. Around and around they rowed. Wind gusted. The sky turned darker.

At last No Name's rowing became erratic. He spoke apologetically to Philip. "I wake Vita." Resting his oars, he stumbled toward her.

Philip's warning system forced his mind into focus. A hot spot! No Name and Vita so close together formed a hot spot! He lurched forward to stop them.

What was he doing? Why hadn't he thought of it? After all the times they had avoided forming a hot spot, now it could save them!

Philip gazed hopefully up at the sky, rested his oars, and crept back to join them. With the three of them, skinny as they all were, they might show up on the scanner. He laughed hysterically, giggling weakly and repeating, "Hot spot! Hot spot!" as he threw his arms around No Name and Vita. He lay between them in the bottom of the skiff.

But neither No Name or Vita seemed to hear. And nothing happened. As time passed, Philip now and then crept back to row them away from shore.

Each time he lay down between the sleeping bodies of Vita and No Name, he hoped again. But, at last, he had to recognize the possibility that even the three of them together were not big enough to make a hot spot. Once again his hopes were dashed. He lay agonizing. Nothing can help us. We are going to die. For a moment he closed his eyes, wondering how long dying would take.

His eyes opened to bewildereing red and green lights blinking over him. The aeroambulance, its underside emblazoned with a huge red cross, hovered just above. Searchlights played on them. Voices discussed them: "Tell the

117

rescue crew the scanner was wrong. It's not just one person. It's three."

Philip struggled up onto his knees. It was happening! They had been found! He lifted his hand and cheered weakly. Beside him, he glimpsed No Name, wide-eyed and frightened, and Vita, half awake, rising, shading her eyes from the searchlight's white glare.

Two uniformed aeroambulance attendants in harnesses dropped from the open door in the bottom of the hovering craft and swayed momentarily over their heads. A mesh net hung between them. Grasping each side of the net, they swung down to where their toes rested on the skiff.

"*Yi!*" said a clear woman's voice from the loudspeaker, followed by what sounded like precise instructions in the language of the Open Country. Philip looked from No Name to Vita, whose faces were alight with understanding.

Philip asked Vita. "What is she saying?"

"She's asking who wants to come first."

"You go," Philip told her. "Then No Name."

He watched Vita and No Name being lifted in the mesh sling to disappear into the square of white light.

It was hard to wait for his turn. As he was lifted he greeted the cluster of faces peering down at him. "Hello!" he said. "Am I ever glad to see you! I thought you'd never find us!"

The faces registered surprise, then beamed at him before turning to one another. "He speaks English!" They all laughed, and a voice explained. "All of the other survivors have been from the Open Country, and none of them speaks English. We Tower people have something to learn from them."

"But my parents? They speak English!" Even though he

was being rescued, fear for his parents still gripped Philip. "They were in an aerocar when the earthquake happened."

A voice said, "They had time to reprogram some aerocars before Central Power went off."

Philip gulped as hope returned. "Then, maybe . . . ?"

"Give us time to hunt for them. We just came. We're from the Eastern Towers."

Hands helped Philip from the sling to join Vita and No Name and guided them to a round table under the bubble at the rear of the aeroambulance. There three glasses of instanutri-shake awaited them.

Philip greedily sucked the eggnoglike drink through his straw. With each sip he felt a river of strength flowing through his body.

As they drank, the crew briefed them on plans for the future. There would be no more walls; the Tower people would try to combine their life-style with the ways of people in the Open Country.

He heard Vita ask about the Scorpions, and the confident reply was, "Oh, they'll reform fast enough. Some of them are already in custody."

Then the talking stopped. Over his drink, Philip gazed into Vita and No Name's smiling eyes. Together they sucked mightily, sharing the delicious pleasure of an instanutri-shake.

When he'd finished, Philip sighed deeply. Safe! They were all safe—he and his good friend No Name and his beloved Vita. Happiness surged through him.

ABOUT THE AUTHOR

MARY W. SULLIVAN is the author of many books for young readers, including *The VW Connection*.

She says about *Earthquake 2099:* "This is my beach I'm writing about. For many years I've walked it, swum in the ocean by it, studied it, loved it, but not without the apprehension all Californians have got to feel about earthquakes—especially now that the San Onofre atomic power plant is located only a few miles down the coast.

"All in all, I've quite enjoyed giving rein to my imagination as well as researching and plotting the story. It seems very real to me—as if it could happen any day."

Mrs. Sullivan has five grown children. She lives in Laguna Beach, California.